EMERGENT

An Anthology of New Voices

Volume One

Including 2026 Pushcart Prize Nominees

Edited by Susan Brearley

Garden of Neuro Institute Publishing

Emergent: An Anthology of New Voices — Volume One

Copyright © 2025 Garden of Neuro Institute Publishing
All rights reserved.

Published by Garden of Neuro Institute Publishing
Poughkeepsie, New York

ISBN: 978-1-962077-16-3

Cover art by Stephanie Wilson
Cover design by Stefanie Morejon

First Edition

Contents

Editor's Note

Finding Voice

The pages that follow represent first steps.

Not first attempts at writing—every contributor here has been wrestling words onto paper for years, some for decades. But first steps into public voice, into saying *this is what I see, this is what I know, this is who I am* and letting strangers witness it.

The Garden of Neuro Institute believes that voice precedes everything. Before you can act with agency, before you can lead, before you can build community, you must first know what you have to say. Writing is where that knowing begins.

Emergent: An Anthology of New Voices collects poetry, essays, and fiction from writers who have spent the past year in workshop together—reading widely, drafting badly, revising relentlessly, and learning to trust their own instincts. The work here is varied in subject and style but unified in intent: each piece represents a writer stepping forward to claim space on the page.

Some of these voices are quiet. Some are loud. All of them are deliciously human.

This is the first volume. There will be more.

— *Susan Brearley*
Poughkeepsie, New York
December 2025

POETRY

Trapped in a Dirty Game

Pascal Gambardella

Beneath the full moon, I took my nighttime walk.
I went past the green forest with the tall oak trees.
My head was in the clouds, engaged in inner talk.
The wind whispered, and I felt its quiet breeze.

Suddenly, something grabbed me from behind.
My hearing was acute, yet only whispers did I sense.
A darkened shadow gripped both my hands in a bind.
Paralyzed with fear, I'll admit to being tense.

I'm trapped in a dirty game I can't afford to lose.
It all depends on what clever play I choose.

A whiff of enchanting perfume caught my attention.
Then, with a needle to the neck, I fell to the street.
I awoke in a dusty room, dark with apprehension.
She sat silently before me, beautiful and sweet.

We sat at a long table with cards dull and shoddy.
Play body-part poker, she said with an evil smile.
Lose a quick hand and I get a part of your body.
What the hell, I thought, and held back my bile.

I'm trapped in a dirty game I can't afford to lose.
It all depends on what clever play I choose.

EMERGENT

A whiteboard was hanging on the dark wall nearby.
With names under the words, "The Dearly De-Parted."
I swear I heard the wheelchairs near us purr and sigh.
Hearing the coffins creak was not for the faint-hearted.

I saw her deal the cards and lift her eyes and sneer.
My hand had three queens and a pair of black nines.
One queen had a missing head; one had no ear.
My last queen's withered face had no vital signs.

I'm trapped in a dirty game I can't afford to lose.
It all depends on what clever play I choose.

She won with four aces and set a hatchet on the table.
How can I clip a nail without taking out some skin?
Thinking of red blood makes me wonder if I am able.
Ah, there is another way, I thought with a grin.

I glanced up. She was smiling without a care.
I removed my sock, put my foot on the chair.
She saw the hatchet sail at her through the air.
There was no one who said I had to play fair!

I'm trapped in a dirty game I can't afford to lose.
It all depends on what clever play I choose.

Rest Well, Dear One

Harrison Prisbrey

Rest well, dear one.
Permit yourself respite
from churning rumination
Engage your breath,
exhaling resistance
Embrace stillness,
the world will mind itself.

Rest well, dear one.
Release bitter thorns
cultivated in distress
Allow your burdens
to fertilize verdant ground
Behold young buds
spring from old wounds.

Rest well, dear one.
Attend to the moment
enfolding before you
Synchronize your heart
with inner melodies
Open your mind
to vibrant possibility

Rest well, dear one.
Claim your birthright

in eternal divinity
Accept your place
as part of an eager universe
Surrender to your
beautiful complexity

Rest well, dear one.
Attune your being
to the cadence of serenity
Submerge completely
into blissful inner depths
Dissolve into oneness,
resplendent in simplicity

Held in the arms of your infinite potential.

EMERGENT

ESSAYS

Cinematic Immunity

Andrew DiMeo

I walked right past security at Newark Airport. Nobody chased me. Nobody yelled, "Stop! What's in the hamper!"

The line of travelers weaving through the movie theater-style retractable belt barriers was too long. I started popping them open and rolled a canvas-lined cart filled with props through the crowd, past the ID checkpoint, and right past the metal detectors. It all happened without thinking, without hesitation.

My walk was confident. Invisible. I disappeared into the sea of travelers, roller bags, pilots, flight attendants, janitors, and food court employees. As families hugged and bathrooms got cleaned, I kept on walking. Unseen.

No one stopped to look at the badge hanging around my neck. Film Crew.

Private Parts.

I was born with cinematic immunity.

My grandfather taught me: "Walk like you belong."

My brother: "Confidence conceals."

My cousins: "Act like you own it!"

It worked on set.

It worked everywhere.

The on-the-job learned invisibility evolved into off-the-job mischief. I used cinematic immunity to sneak into sporting events and see concerts for free. It wasn't as heart rate-increasing as I thought it would be. It was too easy.

Sometimes I had credentials. Sometimes not. After enough shows, wearing the badge became an afterthought.

Abby thwarted herself again, "Damn, I really wanted to bring the dogs to the beach."

"So, let's take them."

"We can't. No dogs allowed."

"Did you check the rules?"

"Yes. You know me."

It's baffling. The whole checking the rules before doing a thing.

"Rules are not made to be followed. They're made to be enforced."

"I know. I know. You say it the same every time."

Today, I'm shocked when I get stopped. One time, Abby and I were in line for a concert at Red Hat Amphitheater in Downtown Raleigh. I was carrying a backpack filled with rain gear, snacks, and mini bottles.

I walked right through, as I usually do. "Hey! Stop! You can't bring backpacks in here!"

No thinking, just walking. No arguing. Confident movements. I turned around, walked out of the security line, and then hurled the bag over a tall metal fence separating the city street from the tree-lined grass field inside the venue. Turned around and walked back through security. No one said a word.

Abby side glanced at me and shook her head. We swung by the concession stand for a few local brews before making our way to the lawn section. Then scoped out a spot, nice and flat, blankets ahead, not lawn chairs, not too much empty space. With our view preserved, I said, "I'm going to look for my bag. Be right back."

I imagine her side of the story is better. What was she thinking? "There's no reason for fans to be walking around in the trees. He's going to get in trouble this time."

What she saw were police officers with flashlights hunting me down. She saw her husband getting arrested. Night ruined. But no. Wait. He's coming back.

"What happened back there?"

"I couldn't find the bag. Then a couple cops came and said, 'Hey, what are ya doing?' and I said, 'I'm looking for my backpack. I can't find it.' Then they pulled out their flashlights and helped me. 'Oh, there it is, up in the tree! Thanks, fellas!' I said. 'You're welcome!' they said."

"They helped you!" Abby's eyes tightened and her lips pursed. Not angry. Something else. Calculating, maybe. Like she was adding up something about me she couldn't put into words and I didn't yet understand.

"That's cinematic immunity."

Her eyes rolled.

We enjoyed the show.

My be-invisible talent wasn't always used for professional purposes and relatively harmless hijinks. In college, I was dirt poor and making my own way. I went too far, and I still got away with it.

I was at the campus bookstore. You know the place, with spirit wear, stickers and license plate frames made for parents. The computer programs for my engineering and physics classes were prohibitively expensive. At the checkout, I stacked the software on the counter—just off to the side. A thousand dollars of CDs in shrink-wrapped cardboard. Microsoft Office. MATLAB. Mathematica. Windows. Norton AntiVirus. CorelDRAW!

The cashier was a student with a 'whatever-man' stoner smirk. Chad. Knew the kid. Had poetry class together the previous semester. I slid my other items, a mechanical pencil, green graph paper, and a chocolate bar, slowly toward Chad. The kind of slow that a magician uses to draw your eyes. Look at this not that. An action that was natural, not planned.

"Need a bag?"

"Nah, I'm good."

"That'll be $5.15," said Chad. He never glanced at the software boxes.

My heart wasn't racing. Should have been. Wasn't.

I handed him a ten, took the change, and placed the pencil, paper, and candy bar right on top of the software boxes. They were mine. Heavy.

Said, "Thanks Chad," then walked out through the security sensors. Nothing beeped. Nobody called after me. Nobody stopped me. Outside, I stuffed everything into saddle bags, kickstarted my motorcycle, and rolled out to my apartment on the east side of Charlotte. The poor side of town. I unwrapped the CDs and installed the software. The chocolate was just the boost I needed to dig into my homework.

Pretty icky behavior, right? Looking back, part of me wants to punch that kid in the face for acting so childish. But then again, I'm impressed by his ability to be resourceful and make his way through school.

Today, I like to pay for my apps and buy the ludicrously priced drinks at the show. I'm not a poor college kid anymore. I can afford it. Even give a big tip to the hard-working souls at the concession stand.

Here I am in my fifties, and I'm still learning. Sure. I know theft is wrong. It's a clear-cut case. But there are still so many places where it never would cross my mind to read the rules.

Abby's all about know-before-you-go. What's the bag size rule? Smaller than a phone? Or a clear plastic backpack? Are dogs allowed? Can we bring in sealed water? What about an empty Nalgene?

One time at a concert, this one in Charlotte, Abby stuffed everything into a micro-sized purse. Security stopped us at the gate. While she got the full inspection, people with clear backpacks filled with bags bigger than hers walked right through. Apparently, a purse inside a clear bag is fine. On its own? Pat-down.

"I'm sorry, ma'am, you have to take this bag outside or check it in with us."

A guy with a huge Dharma Bums rucksack walked right past us without showing a ticket. The security guard yelled after him—'Sir! You need a ticket! Sir!'—then gave up and returned to Abby's forensic inspection.

"You're a magnet for getting searched," I said.

"I know!" She was furious.

"You could have—"

"I know. You're not helping right now."

I kept my mouth shut.

We sorta enjoyed the show.

Thanks to Starlink and Zoom, we're now living a digital nomadic life. We plant our Airstream at RV parks around the country. The list of rules we see is farcical. No "old" campers. No custom rigs. No dog pens. No extendable leashes. No barking for more than ten seconds. No clotheslines, storage tubs, or outdoor decorations. No mats on the grass. No alcohol. No more than one vehicle per site. No laughter after 9 p.m.

"We can't stay there."

"Yes, we can. Rules aren't made to be followed. They're made to be enforced."

"Right. Right."

What do we see at these campgrounds?

Old and custom trailers, dogs off leash, underwear hanging in the sun, multiple cars, people laughing and drinking late into the night.

They get away with it because they're not doing anything wrong.

But if the park doesn't like you, they can enforce the rules.

"They like me. Everybody likes me. We'll be fine."

I've walked this earth for more than fifty years, never worried about the rules. I've had speeding tickets reduced to improper equipment, driven away from what should have been a DUI, and received more warnings than I can count.

It's not a fair world. Part of me always saw it. When getting away with theft as a poor college student, I was also tutoring at-risk students at East Mecklenburg High School, the most dangerous school in Charlotte.

One of my students was on probation. Stole a car. His crime was no worse than my campus store software heist. Being poor. Needing and not knowing another way. It can lead us astray. I can relate to the feeling of desperation, at least for a blink of my life. But while he was on probation, my immunity was paving the way to financial freedom.

Doors opened. I got married, had two children, bought a small house with a white picket fence in a nice neighborhood. I had time to give back. Volunteered. Taught entrepreneurship to ex-cons at the local community center.

But part of my life was an illusion. My marriage crumbled. I lost everything—the house, the savings, the stability. Even my retirement. I was back where I'd been in college. Broke. Desperate. Not sure how to pay the mortgage for a house I didn't live in.

I could have stolen my way out. Walked out of a Best Buy with a PlayStation for the kids. Maybe snagged some small electronics to flip for rent, get a place so I could have visitation. My immunity hadn't expired. The muscle memory still there—the confident walk, the invisible movements, the attitude that says, "this is mine."

But I was forty, not twenty.

Met a friend for breakfast. Asked to sleep on his couch. Called a business partner. Asked for a loan. It took months to get myself into an apartment, see my kids again. We went shopping together for that PlayStation.

Why? Because by then I'd started to understand: the immunity wasn't a superpower I'd earned. It was a hall pass I'd been handed at birth. And my student from East Mecklenburg? He never got one.

I'm fortunate to have found my way back, to volunteer again. I get to coach aspiring entrepreneurs and mentor novice medical innovators, people who have risen through the academic ranks against headwinds I never had to face. And my children, they're grown now, with places of their own.

Sure. I was raised in a business where cinematic immunity was part of the job. I also grew up tall, white, and healthy. I'm not the woman being asked to take her sweater off to pass through security. I'm not a black man getting handcuffed for driving through the wrong neighborhood.

I've never had to think about it. Can't relate to it.

Knowing the rules can make us feel like we're doing something wrong even when we're not. It's like driving through city traffic with police in the rearview mirror. "What's my speed? Is my registration up to date? Did I just swerve over the line?"

Acting guilty draws attention.

"Why did you tell me dogs aren't allowed on the beach? Now I know. Now I'm a beacon of guilt."

Do women and minorities walk around with a beacon all the time? I'd lose years off my life if I had to deal with that kind of stress.

Rules aren't made to be followed. They're made to be enforced.

Easy for me to say.

Hand-Me-Down Splendors

Elle Fredine

When I think of my childhood and the moments woven into the tapestry of my life, among the threads which bind me closest to my family are the memories of our shared clothing—our splendid hand-me downs.

They came to me, imbued with the essence of their previous owner, each with a story to tell. Where it was purchased or made, and why—what makes this one significant.

My first is ever and always the Bunny coat. It was beautiful and soft and white. Real dead bunny pelts went into that beloved coat. It sounds appalling now, a rabbit-skin coat for a child, but that was then and this is now, and all three of us girls loved it in our turn.

Grandpa bought it for my sister when she was two and I still have a photo in some dusty album of her proudly wearing it. It had a decorative tie under the Peter Pan collar with fur pompoms. We would rub the pompoms against our cheeks. Sadly, and in turn, we all-too-soon outgrew the beloved bunnies, and the coat was passed on. By the time it was relinquished to the final sister, the soft pompoms were almost denuded of fur. But my cheek still remember their soft caress.

When I was not much older, my grandma's brown velvet hat held a special fascination for me. It was one of those flattish almost pancakes that ladies of the era would skewer to their heads with a ferociously long, jeweled hat-pin. Three shades of brown it was, from softest fawn to rich chestnut, decoratively stitched ovals seamed together into a jaunty peaked circle, adorned with a pheasant's feather that swept down towards the cheek at a suitably rakish angle.

One of my aunties confided to me those hat-pins were a lady's first line of defense should an ungentlemanly gentleman become too familiar or threaten unwanted attention. I saved her hat for decades, though I never wore it. But whenever we moved house, I would find it in the bottom of my trunk and take it out, remembering Grandma pinning it on as she dressed to leave for work as a telephone operator, way back when.

And then, the red coat. My mother's corduroy car coat. It had a black velvet collar, big black saucer buttons, and wide, three-quarter sleeves with deep, turned back cuffs. Hip-length and elegantly flared, it swirled out when I twisted and twirled. It was the height of high fashion in my delighted, twelve-year-old eyes.

Our school choir had been chosen to participate in a "Thousand Voice Choir" for some fancy-dancey city-wide concert. I understand now, I didn't have a nice "going out" coat, so Mom dressed me in hers. I didn't care. I was in heaven, transported into a stylish, grown-up world, wearing the beautiful, borrowed red coat.

The next item on my list, skipping over a few—quite a few—would be my dad's bell-bottoms. What can I say—it was the sixties, hootenannies and bell-bottoms were de-rigueur for any self-respecting folk singer. Dad had long since given them up in his rise to the exalted rank of Chief Petty Officer. The heavy, white canvas, button-front trousers had languished in a trunk 'til my sister found them. And then, generously allowed me to borrow them for a special high-school assembly in which I was a featured performer—me and my first guitar.

To think my dad was once so slim to fit into the bell-bottoms which now graced the svelte form of his teenage daughter. My sister has a black and white snap of him from his days in uniform—a young, fresh-faced sailor, and he was a handsome devil. She thought it great fun when girls would ask about her oh-so-cute boyfriend. We still giggle about it to this day.

Then there's my wedding dress, bought at a fire sale for my sister, another hand-me-down. It debuted in the aisle of a gothic cathedral. The heavy slipper-satin skirt stood up on its own, but, mercifully, the itchy lace collar had been cut down to a sweetheart neckline for my sister—bless her. I was able to sashay down my bridal aisle without a rash creeping up my neck.

Neither of our marriages out-lasted the dress. The lace and satin confection lingered on in a series of trunks until it was finally misplaced. Lost in one of my mother's moves.

So many images in my mind, so many moments and places—my grandparents walking down the street in the nineteen forties, the black and white photo a time capsule of the stores, the styles, the every-day life. My cousins in the backyard, demonstrating the hula they learned on their Hawaiian vacation, their matching floral, bell-skirted dresses and ballet flats so sixties.

So many memories bound up in borrowed splendor—so many special times and ordinary, unremarkable slices of my every-day, all part of the moments which shaped my life.

The Dark Side of the Human Potential Movement

Pascal Gambardella

This is a cautionary tale for those involved in personal-growth. It is also the story of how a lonely physicist decided he liked people and got hooked on psychology.

Our son Daniel suggested we listen to the six-part podcast, *The Good Cult* (2022). In it, River Donaghey tells the story of Lifespring Inc., a personal growth company. Daniel knew we and other family members had taken the Lifespring training.

Donaghey grew up in a family involved in personal-growth seminars. If his parents hadn't taken an offshoot of Lifespring, he would not have been born. We told Daniel it was the same for us. Without Lifespring, he would not have been born either. Lifespring was an offshoot of the Human Potential Movement. In the 1940s, Abraham Maslow broke from psychology's focus on studying the worst in people. And instead studied what made people thrive. He said,

> *A musician must make music, an artist must paint, a poet must write, if he is to be ultimately at peace with himself. What a man can be, he must be. This need we may call self-actualization... This tendency might be phrased as the desire to become more and more of what one is, to become everything that one can become.*

Maslow's ideas, and the work of others, led in the 1970s to the Human Potential Movement.

John Hanley founded Lifespring in 1974 and dissolved it in the mid-1990s. It was a positive and empowering experience for many attending its trainings. But there were allegations of harm. In 1987, Marc Fisher wrote an exposé of Lifespring in the *Washington Post*. He said,

*...the company's early growth came to a crashing halt in the early '80s
following a rash of bad publicity about psychotic episodes and even deaths
during and after Lifespring trainings.*

In *The Good Cult*, Donaghey suggested Lifespring was seen as a cult
because it pressured participants to enroll others.

Did Lifespring help people? What went wrong? How could the
same organization do so much good for some and such harm to
others? This article touches on these questions from my personal
experience.

Responsibility

Lifespring wanted people to take responsibility for their lives. To
do this, Hanley, Lifespring's CEO, felt participants needed to undergo
a major transformation. This would force participants to leave their
comfort zones and reach their full potential.

Before creating Lifespring, Hanley attended a Mind Dynamics
workshop. There, trainers placed him in a coffin for 12 hours to break
his resistance until he had a breakthrough. This sounds like torture.

Lifespring's way of confronting people *appeared* milder. One
technique was asking a participant to confront their greatest fear. I was
painfully shy toward women when I took Lifespring's advanced
training. They had me write a poem and read it to an unknown woman
in a bar. To me, the experience was both frightening and exhilarating.

Everyone has different fears. According to Donaghey, Lifespring
encouraged someone who could not swim to confront his fear of
water. To do this, he tried swimming in the Columbia River and
drowned. The trainers may have implied that conquering fear was *just*
mind over matter. Yet, they may not have addressed how to conquer
the fear and stay physically safe.

The Lifespring trainings were experiential. In one exercise,
participants had to discuss when they had experienced being a victim.
They were to repeat the same story as if they were responsible. But
what if the person was a rape victim?

Lifespring did not distinguish between different victim experiences. Some people had to relive traumatic events without proper supervision. Others may have felt they were "blamed for being the victim." In 1987, Fisher wrote,

> *Until a few years ago, Hanley preached that everyone is totally responsible for his life; there is no such thing as a victim... Today [1987], Hanley says, 'I have matured in my view.' Instead of telling students they are responsible for everything, Lifespring asks them to 'take a stand' for responsibility, one careful step removed from the old lesson.*

What did Hanley mean by "take a stand?" In his 2012 book, *Are You Getting It?*, he wrote,

> *Any kind of assault, for example, is horrible, but perhaps just as terrible or even more so would be to see someone conclude, as a result of the assault, that there is something wrong with them... Choosing responsibility in cases like these can boil down to choosing to simply accept that the event happened and refusing to give up belief in one's value and the value of engagement in the world.*

This is important. Hanley says to take responsibility for *how you think* about an event. This is something you *can* change.

The victim exercise illustrated a key approach to bringing about change in people's lives. Namely, place people in situations where they can examine their life from another view.

The Bright Side

I took the three Lifespring trainings from March 1980 to July 1980. The decade from 1970 to 1980 was difficult for me. I started it as an army medic in a war zone and finished it as a physicist in a NASA mission control room. Even the month before the training was hard. I was trying to prevent a satellite from becoming space junk.

In February 1980, after we resolved the satellite's problem, I was more than ready for something new. A friend introduced me to Lifespring. Taking the Lifespring trainings had a profound influence on my life. I discovered I liked people, connected with my emotional side, and felt empowered. I found the courage to meet a beautiful woman after the training. She later became my wife.

Lifespring renewed my childhood interest in psychology. I wondered how Lifespring's exercises could change people. I would not be writing this article if I had not taken the training. And I would not be a Neuro-Semantics trainer or life coach. (Neuro-Semantics has its roots in Neuro-Linguistic Programming).

During the first training, I caught a woman who fainted. We became friends, and she introduced me to her husband. He was taking karate. I joined his karate dojo in 1980 and now teach karate and self-defense. We received our first black belts during the same exam in 1999.

Because I found Lifespring so helpful, I was glad to suggest it to my family and friends. My parents, aunts, two siblings and my childhood friend Jerry took the training. I recently asked my sister what she thought of the training, and she had only positive things to say about it.

Jerry came from Boston to Washington, DC, to save me from the Lifespring "cult." He took the first training. In early 2023, I asked him what he thought of the training. He told me Lifespring had helped him escape from his shell. He said he could be more honest and direct at work.

The Dark Side

Now we turn to the dark side of Lifespring. In *The Good Cult*, Donaghey repeatedly described John Hanley as,

> *...a convicted felon and con artist [who] transformed himself into a widely successful new age guru.*

Before he founded Lifespring, Donaghey said Hanley had run scams with his father-in-law. Was Lifespring Hanley's latest scam? I don't think so. Being a life coach, I am hopeful people have the ability to change. The training Hanley developed was effective in helping many people.

What went wrong with Lifespring? Here are two issues. The first comes from *The Good Cult* podcast.

1—Misguided Policy

In 1979, a woman died after she had an asthma attack during a Lifespring training. Lifespring had a policy of checking people's medications at the door. This included the woman's inhaler.

Lifespring viewed medication as a crutch. During an emotional exercise, the woman was having trouble breathing. When a trainer saw her, he asked her to consider what was causing the attack. Then, he walked away from her.

He came back to her later and discovered she was still having problems. According to her sister, he took her out of the training and brought her to the front office. He insisted she did not need her medicine even after she requested it. Her symptoms did not abate, and he pushed her out the door without her inhaler. The woman collapsed on the street and died soon after leaving the training.

I think the trainer's belief may have been:

Physical symptoms are an excuse for avoiding a breakthrough.

I suspect he failed to realize her symptoms could be fatal.

2—Managing Trainers

In his 2012 book, *Are You Getting It?*, Hanley has a short section on "Managing Trainers." He said,

I'd have to admit that a few trainers did go overboard at times, when they felt the ends justified the means... Maybe I should have had zero tolerance when it came to 'renegade' trainers.

He discussed other issues with his trainers, not meeting his standards. Perhaps there was a high-level of self-importance among some trainers. I did not see any mention of how he trained his trainers. Was there a training organization within his company?

The Good Cult did an excellent job of exposing Lifespring's failings. Unfortunately, people died.

The podcast seemed to lose sight of the good things Lifespring did. Lifespring's training helped numerous people, including me, to change their lives.

In January 2023, I was present when Michael Hall, founder of Neuro-Semantics, coached a business executive. Trainers, coaches and business people were present. The client was unreceptive to being coached. Michael told the client why they could not continue with the session. He later emailed coaches, describing the session and what he *would do differently next time*. This is an example of a coach acting responsibly when he realizes coaching itself will not work for his client.

A learning organization has that power. I am not sure Lifespring was one.

The Blackberry Bush

Erica Rose Shannon

My hands curled in red grip around the handlebars, braced against the coastal wind. My cheeks cut through the icy air as my legs pedaled harder. I was picking up speed and feeling a taste of freedom for the first time in my life.

I had no destination but away from, and I knew excitement was bursting me forward into uncharted territory. Overhead twenty-foot redwoods cheered and rustled their green celebration of my passing by, past the small one-room stone church where my mother was married, past the partier neighbor's house, near the old wood mill that had been turning giants into writing paper and house walls for decades.

Back home there had been no place of safety, my drunken stepfather ogling at my budding breasts as he sipped another beer. His temper was reliably unsteady, a souvenir from the Vietnam war.

My grandmother was a mystical creature of deep black eyes and silver hair. She sat for hours at her table beading, breaking the silence only occasionally to hum. During the day she showed me to bead earrings the Native way—always putting the work down when dark thoughts arose. "It goes into the work," she told me. She burned her hair so no one would steal her power.

I had been moody and heated that summer, and my mother's friend Pat told me to ask her later what it all meant. On August 12, 1992 my mother and I laid on our backs under the deep black sky watching the annual meteor shower. I had been holding my bladder as long as could be, not wanting to lose a moment with my mother.

Finally, when I could not hold it anymore, I traipsed inside, untying the thick white band holding up the flap of my bright pink furry pajamas. The tie unbound a flap that allowed for using the toilet without baring one's nudity to the cold of the night. As I wiped, pale and sea shell pink streaked across the toilet paper. I hollered for my mother who came running inside. She laughed with joy and told me I had become a woman, and hugged me in excitement before making me a "moon pad" out of fabric.

It had all been so much to take in, I was longing for adventure but out in the middle of the woods. On the bike I was pedaling to freedom, the wind whipping in my hair.

Suddenly the road turned sharply and my bike wobbled with speed. Time slowed down as I felt my body launch over the handlebars toward a large blackberry bush ahead.

In the center of the bush, I eyed a gap, and I pointed my arms in a dive piercing arrow. As if whisked by an angel, I rose to my feet dusting off my pegged blue jeans. To weave my way out, I swayed my hips, moving forward and back, learning you had to lean toward a thorn to escape its grasp. Any effort to fight, and it had you by the grip.

Safely outside the bush I pedaled home feeling heroic, and since that day, taking on any daunting task has been deemed "jumping in the middle of the blackberry bush."

A Letter to My Loved Ones at My Funeral

Stephanie Wilson

Dear Ones,

I'm dead. It's true. I know you want to expound on my life today, tell stories, hug each other in support. You should, and I hope you do. This is a good thing. But I see two parallel needs today. One, memorializing my role in your world. And two, memorializing your role in mine.

Say anything you'd like about me, be it true or not. Nobody will know the difference. Memory is faulty. History is piecemeal. Stories are personal, and there are many versions, some in competition or contradictory to others. History is a mishmash—a garden of varied experience and interpretation. We can embrace it all, or none of it. We have options in this life. Besides, this variety of rendition is true art, isn't it? Art helps us see the world from as many angles as the sun spouts light.

Today I want you to know how much you meant to me and how grateful I am for you. If I can start my new life as a dead woman this way, I predict I'll be off to a great start. In short, I love you.

What I want more than anything is for you to know how helpful you were to me in my life. I want you to know this because gratitude is the one piece of me that I wish to give eternal life.

First, thank you.

Thank you for your being, for the way you speak, the arch of your eyebrows, and the twinkle in your eyes. This gave me more certainty about the beauty of life than I can tell you. When I looked at your faces through the years, I knew everything would be okay. Or I knew this all was worth it. Or I realized I could push through. Your aging face validated for me life's comprehensive pact. Your baby face confirmed that I wouldn't change a thing—or not many.

If I could award one of your facial expressions a special recognition, I'd give your comedic face—with those naughty eyes, that mischievous mouth—the Mark Twain Prize for Making Me Laugh So Much.

How you managed to be so funny, I will never know. Your humor came at all the strange, unlikely moments, but if you think about it, they were the obvious moments. Laughter is the music of the bones. Our cells know too well this feather-weight perspective is the substance of life. Those high-value times when we giggle come when we step back and look outside ourselves. It's a wide-angle lens directed at the depths and makes life livable—makes it worth it. Your jokes surfaced like a silly pop-up buoy from these deep waters, and it made my life a windfall rather than a regret. If I hadn't laughed all these years, I'd never have seen the sun or the moon or anything but a dour life trope of worrywart.

Second, you are my hero.

You endured while I learned from this. Hardship is the shadow that enables the highlights of our lives. We would never see this life if not for the hard times, and you endured these alongside me. Thank you for modeling life's soup-to-nuts experience. I leave this world holding all of it, not just a filtered slice.

You endured with acceptance—eventually—and this isn't an easy win. I fought my hardship for decades until one day I noticed the patterns in all of us. We have a choice. We have both positive and negative. We have the good and the ugly. We prevail or we don't. Death cares not one bit whether you chose the good over the ugly or whether you chose to stay in the game. It comes to kill you regardless, sorry to say. I realized this and it left me with an easy logic—prevail toward the good. I'd never ever have known this without heroes showing me the way. You guys rock.

Third, you are so beautiful.

I loved the look of you, your skin colors, your unique arrangements of teeth. I loved your tall or bent or wobbly gait. I loved your looks askance and your face as it closed in on itself, sound asleep. I admired your shiny or thinning hair, and for a couple of you, I loved that you had a sense of self to don a wig after your hair was gone. I still can't get your vocal pitch and the sway of your words out of my dead mind.

But your souls were the most cherished things of all—always fresh despite the aging bodies in which they were housed. Since wisdom doesn't develop on a schedule, it was a privilege to witness some of your breakthrough insights, when your mouth hung open and your eyes got murky. Those moments are like the gorgeous butterfly who chooses to fly near you when it could have flown anywhere at all.

They say we're in this together. We still are. It's just that you're with the living and I'm over here with the dead. It's not that different, to be honest, except most people here walk bent over and have thin hair. Plus, everyone has been a recipient of the Mark Twain Prize. It's awesome.

My love and gratitude,
Stephanie

EMERGENT
FICTION

Prayer Hands on the Exit Ramp

Andrew DiMeo

The Chrysler stopped dead on the exit ramp, right where nobody coming off I-40 could see us until too late. I slammed the brakes. Abby's body stiffened, her deep breath audible. It wasn't just us that needed to stop. It was the seven thousand pounds of aluminum we were pulling. A twenty-five-foot Airstream, ass end now hanging blindly on the highway.

My three-quarter ton diesel truck shuddered to a stop. It rocked. Kicked my skull into the headrest. We were six inches from the trunk of the Chrysler. My rearview mirror was useless with the trailer attached. The sideview equally useless. I stared into it, at the blind curve, nervously imagining a semi crushing us from behind.

Cars and trucks had to slow down from 75 to 25 on that ramp. I could feel them before I saw them. The Airstream rocked every time one passed. The massive aluminum Flying Cloud and all her memories swaying like a boat anchored to a dock with each passing vehicle. We were trapped on the dock.

"How do we deal with this?"

"We're too close go around. Backing up is way too risky."

"What are they doing?"

I peered into the rearview mirror and waited. A moment of stillness. No thinking, just actions, I thrust the door ajar, slivered out, and sideways walked toward the Chrysler. Vehicles screamed off the exit, me on a tightrope between my truck and doom.

A former version of me would've strode with broad deliberate steps. Fearless. Wreckless. I'd have been at that driver's window flexing my size and my voice with absolute certainty that I was right. Would've scared some kid into pulling forward, and I would've driven away feeling righteous.

33

My wife would've been silent for thirty miles.
I know because I'd done it before.

* * *

As a young father, I remember driving my son to baseball practice. We were on Ebenezer Church Road. It's two lanes and winding, the state park on one side, children playing in neighborhoods on the other. Cyclists, joggers, and hikers are often making their way along the street. It's perilous. No median. No place to pass.

A car was tailgating. I mean, really pushing at me. I'm the good guy, right? I'm thinking of how hazardous this is for the kids and weekend warriors. So, I tap the brakes a few times to make a point. It doesn't take. I slow down below the speed limit for a minute, then speed back up. Nope. Then, right in the middle of Ebenezer Church Road, I came to a complete stop. Exited my dad-mobile gas guzzler and walked with a wide stance along the yellow stripes to the car.

The driver was a young girl. Highschooler. Maybe college. I gave her my red faced, vein popping rant about how dangerous her actions were. Didn't think about how dangerous my actions were, standing in the middle of the road, creating unexpected, stopped cars on a narrow road, not caring who she could have been, what this could have escalated to.

What a lesson for my son, right? Way to go, dad. Not my finest moment.

That man is still in here. I can feel him in my shoulders, in my jaw, in the way my right hand wants to make a fist sometimes.

Eleven years ago, on a day that haunts me forever, that man lost his temper, not for the last time, but for the time that committed him to change. The Ebenezer Church Road incident? That was years before. Just one of many.

It's taken a decade of therapy, coaching, yoga, meditation, and my wife's unwavering support to find a place of non-judgement. I practice it every day. I practice kindness, gratitude, respect, and love. Every day. It takes longer and longer for the steam to build inside me, for my water to boil over, for my temper to blow. I've wondered lately, is there any steam building at all?

* * *

There in that moment, on an exit ramp off I-40, standing three feet from a Chrysler's tinted-out driver side window, I met the man I've been becoming.

I didn't knock on the window. I didn't broaden my shoulders and expand my chest—body language I learned in a different life.

No thinking. Just actions. The kind practiced. Repeated. Baked into muscle memory. My hands came together. The prayer position. Not because I'm religious. Because it forces my shoulders down, my chest to soften. Because I do it in yoga, after meditations and before meals. Because I can't throw a punch from here.

A Mack truck flew off the exit. Its pressure thrust me a breath closer to the Chrysler, then sucked me back as it passed.

My heart stopped.

My hands still in prayer.

The tinted window lowered.

An imposing man behind the wheel looked first at my hands—then at my eyes—then in his rearview mirror.

"Ah, shit, I'm sorry dude."

He put down his phone and pulled his car forward.

Summer Lightning

Elle Fredine

The old ones tell a story. A youth will come, born of the storm. A maid will take him to her for a single year. And the storm will keep its promise and make fruitful the thirsty land. And the maid will keep her promise. Blood for blood, life for a life. Sealed by the lightning.

I jerked awake, my heart pounding, mouth dry, muscles bow-taut. The dream—fear clawed my throat. *Blood for blood, life for a life.* A year together in exchange for the rain. A promise I'd always kept. Always. *'Til, twenty years ago.* A distant rumble warned of the approaching storm. *No, no—not yet.* But my heart knew and so did the storm.

Beside me, Michael stirred and muttered in his sleep. I lay beside him, my body still as death, longing for the comfort of his arms. For the warm silk of his skin on mine, heart to heart, legs entwined. I ached to rest my head in the perfect hollow where his strong, wind-burned neck met his shoulder. To pretend this was just another night.

Instead, I held my breath 'til he settled, then slid out of bed and padded across the room.

The sprigged muslin curtains fluttered in the rising breeze. Chilled, I rubbed my arms and wondered if I should close the window. Lightning flared low on the horizon, eerie greenish streaks momentarily linking the parched earth to the roiling thunderheads.

The wind caught my hair and dragged it free of its ties. I raked a hand through the silver-threaded chestnut waves to snag the narrow blue ribbon fluttering at my nape, but the wind whipped it away. As I smoothed the unruly tangle back from my forehead, wiry silver strands crackled and clung. Michael had laughed with delight the first time he ran his fingers through my lightning-charged halo, the chestnut curls clinging round his hand.

Images of our beginning tumbled through my mind. My young love cradling a new-born foal, his face alight with wonder. The first time he tasted spring rain, and lay with me under the stars—and still, the fever rush when our eyes meet. In twenty years, that hasn't changed. And in twenty years, I've forgotten nothing of our days. Or our nights. I cannot forget. It's my only gift now—remembering.

Now, Michael's hands bear the scars of twenty years unrelenting toil, coaxing tender green shoots from the dying land. *His hands bring life. Mine, only death. Death for the world.*

Death for him.

I knew, without checking the mirror, new lines had formed by my eyes. Laugh lines? Nothing much to laugh about, now.

Once, there was summer wine, dew-fresh grass beneath bare feet, wild roses and strawberries. Autumn, crisp with scarlet and gold leaves fluttering, tumbling, crunching underfoot. The tang of frost-kissed apples spiced with cinnamon. Long winter nights by the fire. Warm woollen blankets. Hot cocoa and mulled wine, sweet on the tongue.

The huge limbs of the giant oak in the yard below groaned and swayed. Struck by lightning in the last big storm, twenty years ago, one side of the tree'd been sheared away as if by a giant's knife.

Miraculous and stubborn, the tree survived. Dead at its core, the hollow oak still managed to send out green shoots and new leaves each spring and spread its remaining branches to offer welcome shade from the blast furnace of our summer.

And, like the venerable oak, our town managed to cling to life. Surviving somehow on the trickle of water the windmills coaxed to the surface. But the twenty-year drought was winning, killing us off one farm at a time, as one family after another piled their life in a truck-box and fled. Leaving silent, hollow-eyed children with swollen bellies and desiccated twig-limbs to clutch their despairing parents' hands and stare after departing friends from behind dust-smeared windows.

A sudden gust rattled the leaves on the aspen poplars by the barn. They seemed to be whispering to each other, "Maybe tonight—maybe this time?"

I shivered and reached for the sash to close the window.

"You had the dream again."

I jumped. *Dammit.* I turned from the storm outside to face the one within.

Michael leaned on his elbow, his dark hair tousled from sleep. His beautiful hazel eyes, usually so sunny, flashed amber fire. "Didn't you?"

I couldn't lie. I nodded.

Thunder crashed again, louder, closer. Lightning flickered and danced across the brazen sky. And I could see an answering storm rising in Michael's eyes. His brow furrowed, jaw stubborn-set.

Michael swung long legs over the side of the bed and wrapped the sheet, toga-like, around his waist. "It's time." *No—don't say that. I'm not ready.*

He strode across the room, tall and lithe, his curly hair brushing the steep-pitched ceiling. He sank onto the window seat and stared out at the heart of the storm. Then he grasped my arms; pulled me down beside him. I could feel the heat of him through the sheet. Lost in thought, his thumb idly traced the contour of my cheek as he had done so often in the soft silence after love. Then, his eyes searched mine.

"I know you had the dream again. It's time."

It's well past time—twenty years past.

Thunder rattled the window-frame. *Close it. Don't look.* I covered my face with my hands to blot out the storm, to hold back the unshed tears burning my eyes. Fighting to deny the awful truth.

Lightning cracked, so near the house, I saw the glare of its spiking fire through my tight-squeezed eyelids. *Please, I'm not ready. I can't—I can't breathe.*

"It's time." Michael's steel-edged command cut through the storm's clamour.

I stared, after twenty years finally seeing him. My beautiful love. *He knows. He's always known. Even before I told him my dream.*

Salt-drops rolled down my cheeks, bitter on my tongue. I slid to my knees, sobbing, and wrapped my arms around his legs. The words ripped from my heart. "Please. I can't. I can't do it again."

Twenty years I'd had with Michael. Twenty precious, stolen years and not one drop of rain had fallen. Still, I couldn't give him up. *I won't—not again.* Everything could die. I wanted everything to die. Then I would die too, and it would be over.

Michael raised me from the floor. Brushed my forehead with his lips, soft as a butterfly's wing. Cradled me against his chest, his breath warm in my hair. Gradually my racing heart slowed. Matched his heart's steady rhythm.

"I stayed for you," he whispered.

"But—" I tilted my head back. Gazed at his face, taut with an expression I couldn't quite read.

His generous mouth twitched. "You are not the only one who loves."

"You were supposed to go back twenty years ago." My cheeks burned. "I couldn't give you up."

Michael looked away. "You couldn't help but love me. The storm made me for you."

My heart gave a painful jerk. "The storm—made you?"

Michael's hazel eyes returned to mine, glowing with the light of the summer sun. "Yes. The storm made me—and the storm is me. But it did not know I would want to stay."

I pulled away, chilled to my core. *His words echoed in my head—'The storm made me, the storm made me.'* But, though my mind heard his words, my heart denied them.

"No—no. You're flesh and blood. A man, the same as any man." *But not the same, never the same, for you are my only beloved.* "You cried for joy the first time you heard a mockingbird's song. You always leave your socks under the bed. You—The storm stole you from some grieving mother—"

"No, my love." Michael's smile was tinged with sadness. "I am flesh and blood and bone and sinew. My heart yearns and breaks like yours. But I am born of the storm. And to the storm I must return. And you, Amiah, beloved—" His hand cupped my cheek. "You are the keeper of the promise."

His words pierced my soul. I wanted to hurt him as he was hurting me. "You're not the first." My voice sounded cold, distant—*My bones are ice. I am hollowed out and my heart is turned to stone.*

He nodded. "Nor will I be the last. But I will always be."

A stubborn flicker of hope stirred, refused to be stilled. "What do you mean, 'I will always be'—will you come back? Is it always you who comes back?"

Michael shook his head. "No, beloved. We can come only once. But the storm—"

"No." I wrenched away. "I don't want the storm, I want you."

Michael grabbed my arms and tried to pull me close. I screamed and slammed my fists into his chest again and again, my fury matching the storm.

A sheet of lightning flashed across the sky, enveloping us in its white-hot glare. And in an instant, we were standing under the oak tree.

It was my dream. Michael, twenty years ago, beautiful in his youth and strength. A young David facing Goliath, shining white against the oak tree in the dark heart of the storm.

I screamed his name, my cry barely audible over the shrieking wind.

The knife gleamed in my hand, raised high. "No—take me—"

But there was no bargaining with the storm. The lightning claimed the knife, blazed a trail of fire towards my love. Then, a blinding flare. Michael cried out in agony as the light consumed him. His skin flamed and blackened, shredded away in a flurry of grey flakes borne on the wind. His bones glowed white, incandescent, then crumbled to dust. The stench of burnt-offering hung in the air.

As the cold rain began to fall, soaking the scorched, thirsty ground, I turned towards the white clapboard farmhouse, in my mouth the taste of ashes, my body heavy as death. I knew, without looking, my hair was dark again, my face unlined.

"Is it you?" His voice was so young.

Not again. I can't do it again.

A blackened, barren landscape filled my mind. No farms, no life, no suffering children. I opened my arms and welcomed the desolation. I was fading, dissolving. And he spoke again—

"Are you the one?"

Everything or nothing. That was my choice.

For one frozen moment, life and breath and sense stopped.

Don't look back. But all the pain to come could not quench the whisper of hope rising in my breast—a tiny, fluttering bird.

I turned.

Standing where the blasted tree had been, a sturdy sapling raised its leafy head. And under the tree, a beautiful youth with autumn hair and lightning in his golden eyes.

"Are you the one?" he asked again.

My throat closed. I nodded.

He held out his hand. Long-fingered, beautiful. Unmarked by this life.

I knew he wasn't Michael. Knew he couldn't be—still I searched his eyes, trying to surprise some small piece of my lost love in those golden depths.

He cocked his head to one side. "Do you know me?"

Nothing—there was nothing of Michael in these eyes. I closed my eyes against the prick of bitter tears.

Warm fingers stole into mine. He took my hand in both of his and placed it on his chest. And in the measured beat of his heart, I heard the echo of Michael's voice "My heart yearns and breaks like yours. It loves as deep and long as yours."

I saw the coming year. Dancing under the grape arbor in the morning mist, our bodies pressed close in the perfect harmony of lovers. Sharing a warm, crusty, loaf fresh from the oven, thick-slathered with butter and black-berry jam. Sugar cookies cooling on the kitchen sill. Heads together of a long winter's eve by the fire as we searched out pieces of a "Where's Waldo" jigsaw puzzle. Laughing at our lop-sided snowmen 'til our bellies ached and carolling off-key to the cat family in the barn, fluffy grey mites with pale pink noses curled, trusting, in our mittened hands.

I opened my eyes. Breathed deep of the cooling air. *Life will go on. We will go on.*

"I know you," I said.

He smiled like the sun coming out, and my heart shattered in a million pieces. For I knew I would love him. And when our year was done, I would bring him to the oak tree and return him to the storm. The parched land would live again. And my heart would die with each new love.

The old ones tell a story. A youth will come, born of the storm. A maid will take him to her for a single year. And the storm will keep its promise and make fruitful the thirsty land. And the maid will keep her promise. Blood for blood, life for a life. Sealed by the lightning.

Governor Alarmed by Censored Ink, Stiffens His Spine

Pascal Gambardella

The state legislature overruled Governor Roger Dim's veto of a vague book-banning law. The law empowered Censored Ink, the shelf-control group. Dim had not paid enough attention to the "book banning minority" in his state. Censored Ink was unpredictable, and he was unsure of their next move. He needed a plan to avoid losing the next election because of a potential majority backlash.

He remembered Asimov's "perfect laws" for safeguarding humans from AI robots. Asimov's stories highlighted unexpected outcomes of these laws. Dim wondered how to discover his book-banning law's unanticipated consequences.

Censored Ink Targets The Big Bang Theory

Arthur Chill banged the gavel and called the meeting to order. "I propose banning the Big Bang theory. Let's remove books on it from all schools and public libraries. It is too incredible for any sane person to believe and will confuse young adults."

Silvia piped up, "What a novel proposal. The 'Big Bang Theory' confuses me too. Why should I watch someone write equations on TV? It is like watching a book being printed."

Chill replied, "It's not the TV program. I want to ban the theory *that our universe exploded into existence 13.8 billion years ago*. Physicians believe time began then, and the universe came from nothing. It sounds too weird and violent for kids. Those cosmetologists can create havoc in our children's lives."

"*Cosmetologists?*" Silvia murmured. "Aren't they supposed to fix bad hair days?"

Chill said, "Our librarians must redact 'Big Bang' from school dictionaries or ban them. My *Oxford English Dictionary* lists *Big Bang* as an example of *big*." Chill pulled the school's *American Heritage Dictionary* from the bookcase near him. He looked up at the word *big* and breathed a sigh of relief. Its definition did not include the *Big Bang*. Then he looked further along the page and groaned. Unlike the *Oxford English Dictionary*, the term *Big Bang* had its own entry. He read,

> *...the universe originated ~20 billion years ago from the violent explosion of a small agglomeration of matter...*

Hester, the lone science geek and former A-student, said, "The dictionary is 6.2 billion years off. We should focus on teaching critical thinking theory. We can ask students how they would handle errors in books. Or, ask them how to think about addressing major problems, like climate change."

She went on, "Let's discuss banning dictionaries. Michigan prisons banned the Spanish dictionary. The prisons think Spanish is a *very obscure language*. They did not want people knowing Spanish to cause disruptions. Didn't they realize Spanish is the second most spoken language in the US?"

"Arthur," she asked, "are you treating cosmology as a *very obscure field?* Where is critical thinking when you need it the most?"

Hester argued with Chill for a few minutes more without success.

No one knows how Hester got into their group. They suspected she was the token-compromise. Yet, she was in the minority, and no one listened to her. Hester believed in age-appropriate limitations for topics like sex. In other areas, she felt the group had gone too far. Unlike the pages of a book, the world was not black and white.

Harry suggested they ban all theory. He felt people should rely on facts and practical experience. He mentioned the famous investigator, Friday something, who said, "Just the facts, ma'am."

Chill said, "Harry, good point. Let's shelve it until our next meeting."

Dim Seeks Help and Gets Pearls of Wisdom

Governor Dim went to the local Department of Unanticipated Consequences, or DUC. He was desperate and hoped DUC could help him. He met Pearl, the DUC lead, and said, "I am in a real bind and need to show my constituents I have a spine. What is your assessment of the consequences of censorship in our state?"

Pearl said, "A close relative of mine is a member of Censored Ink. She stayed in state hotels and found two banned books in nightstand drawers. The first was a Big Bang book, *A Universe from Nothing,* by Lawrence Krauss. Your state banned it." The book contains a note signed by the "Band of Astro-Nerdy Guys—or BANG." It says,

> *Many religious people accept the Big Bang theory. Georges Lemaître, a priest, proposed the Big Bang theory in 1931. Twenty years later, Pope Pius XII said the Big Bang theory is not in conflict with the Catholic idea of creation. In contrast, atheist scientists condemned it, claiming it had "creationist overtones." Yet, since then, evidence from many areas supports the theory.*

Pearl said, "We discovered a former high school astronomy teacher leads BANG. The school dismissed him for having students read *The Lonely Hearts of the Cosmos* by Dennis Overbye. Who knew the school would forbid a history book that mentions the Big Bang?"

She continued, "The second book in the drawer was the Bible. BBC News had a report about the Utah school district removing the Bible from elementary and middle schools. The ban was a consequence of the new Utah censorship law and a complaint from one parent. It violated their rules of *vulgarity and violence.* This can happen in your state."

Pearl looked directly into Dim's eyes and said, "The new law is scaring librarians and science teachers, leading to a shortage. Your state is fostering division over critical thinking and collaboration."

An associate handed Pearl an urgent report from her investigator. She read it to Dim.

> *Censored Ink sent its Shelf-Patrol police to take away all Big Bang books from high schools. The police went overboard to ensure a thorough*

job and took all physics and astronomy books. Science teachers are in an uproar!

Students were calmer. It seems BANG set up read-easies at hidden locations. Read-easies provided access to banned books, like speakeasies did for alcohol during Prohibition.

BANG held Bang-a-Thons to organize book lectures to celebrate forbidden science. It also gave shy science geeks an opportunity to mix with the opposite sex.

Dim felt stupefied. Pearl smiled and said, "That is a blot on Censored Ink's reputation."

The Bean Fionn

Kathy Minicozzi

Keira removed her shoes and stockings and stood up to feel the leaves between her toes. She smiled as she squished a few of the leaves with her two big toes, leaving big green spots on her feet. Her mother would scold her, but Keira had endured many scoldings. She wasn't afraid. She began to walk toward the stream, which lay a short distance ahead.

The day was warm and clear, with bits of sun escaping between the leaves of the overhanging trees, warming Keira's shoulders. The air carried the woody scent of the trees, shrubs, and leaves, as well as the rumble of the stream and the squawks of a gaggle of geese in the distance.

Keira stepped cautiously over leaves and pebbles, being careful not to cut her feet on any sharp rocks. She almost lost her balance once but caught herself. Mother always told her if you stumbled it was the angels telling you not to go any farther. How could she not go any farther, though, on such a beautiful day, after she had gone to great lengths to slip out of the house unseen? When she reached the stream, she knelt on the soft bank and looked into the water.

The water was so clear that Keira could see not only a distorted reflection of herself, but also every colored rock in the stream bed. She giggled at the reflection, then reached down with both hands, scooped up some water, and drank it. The water was frigid, and it tasted better than the well water they had at home. She took another scoop and drank it as well.

Keira became aware of a strange silence. She could no longer hear the geese. She wondered why no birds were calling in the trees. She had been excited about her clandestine walk to the stream, and she had not noticed the absence of birds until now. There was only the sound of the stream, growing louder.

The sun, which had been shining through the trees, slipped behind a cloud, and semi-darkness enveloped the place. Keira shuddered.

She began to feel the presence of something. She looked up and saw, across the water a little way upstream, a tall, auburn-haired woman in a long, white dress. The woman was too far away for Keira to see her features, but she appeared to be beautiful. She was standing shin-deep in the water. Keira had heard of the Bean-Fionn, who seized children when they went too close to a river or stream and dragged them under the water, to their deaths. She wondered if this was one of those dreaded fairies. She stood up, picked up her shoes and stockings, and backed away, leaving a short distance between herself and the water. She was too curious to leave but stood and watched the distant figure.

The woman in white began to wade downstream. Her steps were easy, as if she were walking on a paved street. The water moved to make way for her. When she was directly across from Keira, she began to cross the stream. When she reached the bank, she stopped, as if unable to go any farther. Her flowing white dress was dry. She smiled at Keira.

"Hello," said the woman. "I've been waiting for you. Welcome."

"Hello," said Keira. "Who are you?"

"I am the good spirit of the water," the fairy answered. "If you come with me, I will bring you into a place of enchantment, where you will have good things to eat and plenty of woodlands where you can play forever. The weather is always pleasant there, and there are beautiful flowers and lovely music. You can dance all day long, and you will never have to work."

Keira stood without moving. She wanted to believe what the fairy was telling her, but something held her back.

"I see that you doubt me," said the fairy. "Don't be afraid. I will never hurt you."

The fairy looked fixedly at Keira, and her eyes began to emit a soft glow, which grew in intensity until Keira's mind and spirit were pierced and enveloped by it. Keira began to stumble toward the water.

"Come, come," said the fairy, and her voice was the most beautiful sound Keira had ever heard. The fairy began to sing in tones no human voice could produce, and Keira felt as if she no longer had control over her feet; a power beyond her was moving them. "I am under the power of a Bean-Fionn," she thought, "I feel no fear because she has me under a spell."

All of a sudden, another sound broke through the fairy's song.

"Keira! Where are you? K-E-I-R-A! Dear God, help me find her!"

It was the voice of Keira's mother.

The Bean-Fionn stopped singing, angry over the interruption.

"Go away! I don't want you here!" shrieked the fairy. Keira stopped and turned around to see who was calling.

"Keira! Answer me! Keira!"

"Mother!" shouted Keira as loudly as she could. "Help me! A Bean-Fionn has me, and I can't get away!"

Mother and Keira shouted back and forth until Mother burst through the nearby trees, ran to Keira, and clasped her in a tight embrace.

"Let her go! She's mine!" shouted the fairy.

"No!" said Mother. "I'd rather you drown *me*. Leave her alone!"

Mother began to murmur a desperate prayer. Keira joined her. As they continued to pray, the fairy morphed into a hideous old hag. She gave a long, loud wail and disappeared.

Keira could move again. She kissed Mother and said, "Oh, Mother! I will never slip away from home again!"

"Well," said Mother. "I would punish you, but you have had enough. I am going to give you an early supper and put you to bed. You have had a bad fright."

"Will you keep the spirits away from me?"

"Don't worry, Baby. I won't let anything hurt you again."

Fragments of a Small God

Stefanie Morejon

01/

It happened pretty quickly once I made up my mind. Call it chance, or call it destiny—but that girl smelled like pizza, beer, and mischief, and I just couldn't help myself.

I haven't always been able to see the future—sometimes I see flashes of what could be, but don't know quite what to call it. That day, though, it came into focus and I heeded the call: she was going to be the one.

I sidled over to where they were standing, hopeful by nature but made wary by the streets. There were three of them, all tequila-fueled bluster and erratic movement, but I saw an opening and made my move.

Cautious but determined, I peered around the side of the car and waited for her to notice me. You can tell a lot about a person by the way they react to you, whether they're nervous and skittish, or welcoming and open. I'd been burned plenty of times before, but that's to be expected when you cut your teeth in dumpsters and back alleys, begging for scraps and taking what you can wherever you can get it.

It wasn't always this way. I lived in a house at first, warm and comfortable, with plenty of soft places to rest and my siblings all around. There were a lot of us, but we made it work when it mattered, sharing our food and our mother as best we could.

But then I made one of those wrong choices that feel right at first. He left the door open, and the threshold smelled like a freedom I wasn't prepared to resist. Out I went, curiosity getting the best of me like it so often did, and by the time I found my way back, the door was locked and I was on my own.

Turns out what I thought had been wrong ended up being right, but I didn't know that yet. All I knew was that the girl they called Esti seemed open, and that would have to be enough.

I crept closer, holding my breath.

She turned, and her eyes lit up.

"Hey, kitty... you hungry?"

Yes. Yes, I was.

02/

Esti hadn't invited me into her bed, but she didn't try to stop me either. That was all the permission I needed. The couch was comfortable, far more comfortable than the streets had been, but it was lonely.

We woke up at the same time, groggy and disoriented, shy and uncertain. I braced myself to run, worried that she'd regret the decisions her tired mind had made the night before, but she smiled and turned toward me, her hand gently cupping my face.

"Good morning," she smiled. "How did you sleep?"

Gloriously. Exuberantly. Warm. Happy.

"Are you ready for breakfast?"

Yes. Of course. Always. What's breakfast?

We stretched and padded over to the kitchen, still aware of each other's unfamiliar mass, bodies bouncing off each other as we crowded into the small space built as an afterthought that had the audacity to call itself a kitchen, trying to figure out where we best belonged.

The day unfurled naturally after that. She worked, typing frantically into a metal box while telling me about her research and her ability to procrastinate. I lounged under a sunbeam illuminating the corner of the couch that would eventually become my spot, dozing off in the long periods of silence between her words. She played music, soothing and calm, and before I knew it the sun had gone down again and I was still safe.

I could get used to this.

I wandered around her space, cautious and curious. It wasn't large—not like that first house, the one from a previous life that I had

walked out of on my own steam and always dreamt of returning to—
but it was warm, and I was welcome, and that was more than I could
say for all the places I'd been in the time between.

I heard her on the phone one day, asking if anybody knew where I
had come from, or where I could go. I panicked, ran through the house
like a petulant child, leaving behind a wake of destruction that might
remember me when I was gone. How could she not want me to stay?

I made myself useful while I waited to be cast out, sweeping the
corners of dust and crumbs and tucking loose items away so they could
not be seen. I was careful not to get too comfortable, always sure in
those days that it would be my last with her, but the inevitable goodbye
never came. She stopped calling after a couple of weeks, and I found it
easier to relax.

"I guess you're stuck with me, buddy. Should we go get you a bed?"

She came home that day, backpack bursting with brightly colored
toys, packets of food I would eventually learn how to open on my own
when she was gone too long, and a huge smile on her face. She ran
back out to the car, came back wrestling a giant bed, and presented it to
me proudly.

"This is for you, Niko. Do you want to see all the rest of your
things!?"

Once I understood that I was staying, I stopped sleeping with one
eye open and started to claim my space. The left side of the couch
became mine, as did the right side of the bed. I began to accumulate
things, and places to put them. I had a favorite pillow on our bed, and a
preferred bowl.

I'd never had places to call my own before, and it was a rush. I
woke up every morning excited just to look at everything, to claim
them, to touch them and move them at will, knowing they'd still be
there if I closed my eyes. I had found a place I belonged that was mine,
and I never wanted things to change.

The day she explained that we had to move, I did my best to talk
her out of it. It's hard to explain how much walls can come to mean to

somebody who's never had them, how anxiety can set in at just the thought of going back out into the unknown.

Her mind was made up, though, as well as the landlord's.

"I'm the only one who's allowed to be living here, and he knows you've been here, too. I love this place, but we can't stay."

My eyes turned down, then. As soon as I understood that I was the problem, I knew the time had come for me to leave. It was my fault; she shouldn't have to leave just because of me.

She started packing up boxes, and I started making my own plans. It hadn't been that long; maybe my friends were still around, and would know a safe place where I could go until I figured things out. I could be strong. I had been strong before. I'd gotten used to the comforts of a home, but I hadn't forgotten how to live on my own. The streets, for all their activity, were the loneliest place I could imagine, but they weren't her cross to bear.

Then, one night, while she was packing my things into their own box and I was trying to sneak them out one by one while she wasn't looking, she said the words I've never forgotten to appreciate the most.

"Don't worry, buddy. I would never leave your favorite toys behind!"

"Oh," I thought to myself, warmth spreading through me like an invasion. "Oh."

03/

The new house took me a whole week to explore, room by room, before I grew weary of its walls and gave in to my urge to explore the grounds beyond.

The first day, I wandered over to the neighbor's yard, inspected his garden grown lush under the summer sun, and laid down on the border of our properties to watch the birds make their way through the afternoon. The outside wasn't as scary when you had a place to go at the end of the day.

I spent more time in the neighbor's yard, let him chase me around the rose bushes, and wandered farther and farther away as time went on and my confidence grew. I would run into old friends sometimes, their territory expanded in my absence, tried to convince them to come back with me, but they scoffed and called me "owned" like it was a bad thing.

Having a home isn't the same as being owned. I could do whatever I wanted, and I always had a warm place to sleep at the end of the day. There were people in every room, always happy to see me, and new friends would walk through our front doors at all hours, dancing and drinking and happy to lay down on the floor with me for a cuddle.

"The people are the problem," Old Tom insisted, but I found that I didn't mind their happy smiles and friendly hands, even when they were erratic. Sure, Esti forgot to feed me sometimes, but there was always food to be had in the kitchen, and someone was sure to come along eventually and realize that my bowl was empty.

I started roaming farther and farther away, confident in my ability to find the house unchanged when I returned, sure that one of our roommates would always be around to let me back in when I scratched at the back door. Esti put a piece of fabric around my neck one afternoon, kissed me on the forehead, and told me it was just in case.

I was curious about the synagogue, but I'd been turned away twice; I knew they weren't likely to let me in, me not being like them. I didn't know much, yet, but I knew this was a space closed to the rest of the world, set apart in some way. I sat far enough away to remain hidden by the tree at the edge of the road, and watched as the people filed in and stayed.

That many people don't go into a single place by accident. What was happening inside those walls?

I crept closer than I had dared before, after the doors had closed but well before I knew they would be opening again, and held my breath as I tried to listen for a sign that it was worth the effort of finding a way in. There was singing, and the hum of voices in unison, and I crept forward in a trance.

It happened all at once, as these things tend to do.

Someone shouted behind me, and I started to run. One second, I was on firm ground, sprinting along the sunbaked stone of the synagogue's walls, and the next I found myself landing in a heap at the bottom of a hole deeper than any I'd seen before. My eyes adjusted quickly, the sliver of light from above enough for me to see that I was in a narrow space, not much wider than I was, and alone. I scratched and scrabbled, but I couldn't get out.

It was quiet for a while before I started hearing people talking in hushed tones on the other side of the wall. I was quiet at first, afraid to be discovered, but hunger was starting to get the better of me and I knew I had to make myself known. My voice grew hoarse, raspy from calling out into the darkness for someone to come help; I could hear them, just through the stones, but nobody came.

Would I ever see Esti again?

It took three days and a whole team of strangers with bright lights and loud demands. They tried to lift me from above, struggled to get the ropes around me, but I wasn't about to help them without knowing who they were and what they would do to me once they found me out.

Eventually, they had to bring in a demolition crew. The noise was deafening, everything rumbling and shifting in the darkness I'd become accustomed to. The light, when it finally found its way through, blinded me just long enough that I was too disoriented to evade the nets they threw around me.

I tried to escape, of course, but the man with the gruff voice had held me tight around the shoulders, and all I could do was imagine what horrible things they would do to me for sticking my nose where it didn't belong. Would I be punished for my crimes? Worse?

When we pulled up outside our house, I was overjoyed. Esti came running down the street, bag open and books dropping in her wake, shouting my name through the happiest of tears.

"It's a good thing little Niko had a collar. We would've had to take him to the shelter if we hadn't seen the number."

I didn't go outside much after that, and never alone. Why leave a perfectly good home when you have it?

04/

Esti met Cate in the summer, brought her home late one night, shouting in whispers tinged with something I'd never heard before in her voice. They sat together for hours in the dimly lit living room, talking and drinking out of bottles, the mirth of recognition a palpable hue in their eyes. I was used to a revolving door of strangers by then, but this felt different, and I wasn't sure if I liked it.

That first night, Cate stayed. They climbed into our bed well after the sun had risen, their sleepy breathing mingling together for the first time. She was in my spot, but I hadn't been asked to join, and I was livid. I spent the night sulking in the shadows, keeping an eye on her, watching for signs of danger.

I was careful, whenever she was around, not to drop my guard.

Cate became a fixture in the house, spending more time in it as the days wore on, and we developed a rhythm. We would catch up on our programs and take long naps together in the middle of the day, waking up and stretching in time to welcome Esti home.

Those first few years we were together were decadent. There were cheese plates and forgotten glasses of wine, elaborate dinners and music at all hours. I stopped being wary, gave in to the familiarity of another set of hands. I learned to make noise from my favorite spot on the bathroom rug when Cate would stumble into the room, fumbling in her blindness, and she learned how to scratch the spot under my ears that I loved. Esti had never been happier, and her joy covered us all like a blanket.

They went out a lot those first few years, always coming home to me in some form of disarray. Messy, but as happy to see me as I was to see them, even if they had been gone for days. I didn't mind their absence so much, eager as I was to celebrate their return.

By the time we outgrew the cramped, one-bedroom apartment and started looking for a bigger space, the three of us were inseparable. I was surprised to find that I wasn't worried this time, about being left behind and forgotten.

One night, they came home laden with empty cardboard boxes, excitement thick around them, and gathered up all the blankets and pillows in the house.

"Happy birthday, buddy! Let's build a birthday fort!"

By the time the sun came up through the fabric of our makeshift walls, I'd never felt more loved. I'd thought about what Old Tom had said plenty of times, especially on the days when my breakfast was late and I was left to my own devices, but maybe he wasn't so wise, in the end. I'd have a whole lot more freedom if I still lived on the streets, but I wouldn't have these humans—my humans. People who loved you weren't scary, even if strangers could be a mixed bag.

I had a family that knew my birthday; I was the luckiest cat in the world.

05/

They'd been whispering about moving again for weeks before it finally happened.

I'd come to learn that this process was part of our lives. We'd lived in three houses in as many years, and I was confident by then that I wasn't going to be forgotten. They'd take me with them, no matter where they went.

What I didn't expect was the month Esti and I spent away from Cate, with the old man who took joy in throwing his shoe at me whenever I tried to help him with the cooking. There were plenty of new rooms to smell and explore, but I missed the familiarity of my home, and Cate most of all.

I'd hear her voice, sometimes, extending out through the phone Esti would place in front of me every night before bed. A tinny reproduction, hardly as good as the firm realness of her arms wrapped around me and always leaving me feeling lonelier than I'd started, but I was grateful for the connection, however fleeting.

There was another animal in the house, too—a slobbery, furry beast whose tail only knew excitement and whose paws could be described as bungling at best. He was harmless enough, if you could get past the utter lack of elegance, but I hated the nights when he would clamber into our bed, taking the space where Cate should have been.

Little did I know that my trial had only just begun. Esti packed me into the car one morning, the sky foreboding, and we drove for an hour until we arrived at our destination, a cold, sterile room where I was poked and prodded and manipulated until I passed whatever test I was being forced to take. We left that day with a binder of paperwork and considerable trust broken between us, but I was glad when we finally ensconced ourselves once again in the security of Esti's childhood bedroom. Safety, at last.

That's when she started packing.

The next thing I knew, I was woken up from a nap, hustled into my travel bag, and driven to the loudest place I'd ever been. There were more people in this place than I had ever seen in my life, all of them rushing past like they were running away from something dangerous.

It was hot in the plane, especially in the space I'd been unceremoniously shoved into in the flurry of activity. I couldn't see anything except Esti's feet, couldn't hear myself think over the din of the chattering and the loud, angry noises that only grew in intensity when we started moving. On the back of the day I had already had, I was about done with all of this.

I waited what felt like several lifetimes, until everything was quiet and the hum of the engines had started to feel like a permanent fixture, before I made my move. Carefully, quietly, I pulled and tugged at the zipper until it gave way, poking my head up to get a better idea of what I was up against. There were more legs—and unfamiliar ones—but I didn't sense any danger in their movement.

Esti was asleep, buried under a blanket, and I remained undetected. The lights were dim, the coast was clear, and I knew the time had come for me to take matters into my own hands.

I leapt, using the closest pair of legs to claw my way out of the tight space, and heard a man yell in my periphery as I hurtled down a tight aisle. I dodged right, came across a child with eyes bigger than a kitten's who started to scream, and climbed higher.

It took four grown men and a flight attendant twenty minutes to wrestle me to the ground before I was dropped back into Esti's waiting arms. We waited patiently while she was admonished, and she put me back into the carrier she kept on her lap for the rest of the trip.

"Good boy," she whispered through the netting, dropping treats inside through the open zipper. "You have to stay in here, but you're a very good boy."

06/

The years Cate and Esti rarely left the house were the best ones of my life.

We'd been in the apartment for longer than I could ever remember being in one place, and I loved the routine of it. Every morning, I'd sit on my windowsill and look down at the miniature people below, count the birds along with my blessings, and wait patiently for them to wake up and prepare my breakfast.

After breakfast, one or both of them would leave, for "work" I'd heard them call it, though the jury was out on what that actually entailed. I'd gotten used to being alone in the afternoons, and had even started to enjoy that time, the house quiet and nobody to say no if I happened to jump on the counter and help myself to a crumb or two.

Every evening, I'd welcome them back and take my place on top of the refrigerator, overseeing the preparation of dinner and snacks before we all settled down in front of the television, cuddled together on a single cushion of the couch.

The Good Time started on a Monday. Nothing felt wrong, not really, but I noticed that they didn't leave for work at the usual time. They didn't leave the following day, or the day after that, and Esti started to spend a lot of time wiping down the boxes they would bring into the house. When they didn't leave for five days, I knew something was up, but I was too busy luxuriating in their undivided attention and the scraps of bacon they would leave behind on the kitchen counter.

There was a lot of stress hovering in the corners of the house at that time, but also a lot of music. Cate brought a guitar home one day in a huge box I couldn't wait to play with, the aura of excitement coursing through the house, heady and thick.

"It's for Esti's birthday, Niko. We can't open it yet!"

I waited an eternity for that box to come out of the closet Cate had stashed it in. When it did, I wished it could go right back into the box it came out of. The cacophony of it was awful. I did my best to be supportive, but even the best of us have our limits. I took to leaving the room whenever I saw Esti settling down to play, hoping she wouldn't ask me what I thought, sure that this would be the day my eardrums would shatter beyond repair.

She was persistent, I'll give her that. I thought I would have to move out when more instruments appeared in the house and they both started plucking at the strings, manifesting a discordant harmony no manner of walls were thick enough to drown out.

Eventually, our collective patience paid off. The melody started to reveal itself, first in fits and starts, and then in blocks of beauty amidst the noise. Cate's fingers, once she learned how to use them, traveled over the strings with a mind of their own, plucking harmonies out of the ether, and I loved to lay next to her and listen.

I stopped leaving the room, started looking toward the guitars in the corner, hoping they'd be inspired to pick one up. Whenever I wasn't feeling my best, which had started happening more often than not, their gentle strumming was the only thing that could help me get to sleep.

Pretty soon, I couldn't remember what the house had felt like before the music. It's something, really, to recognize you've found your place in real time. I'd been waiting for this kind of home for my whole life, hoping to feel like I belonged, like I mattered.

Like I was home.

07/

The first time I turned yellow caught us all by surprise.

It was summer, the days steamy and nights long. The heat was relentless, but we ate popsicles and ice chips to lessen the intensity of the heatwave, spent the nights sitting by the open window, and drew the curtains to fend off the sun. We'd gotten into the habit of sleeping in separate areas of the house, knowing that we'd be drawn to each other in our somnolent states and that it would make waking that much more unbearable.

It was on one of these nights that I woke up suddenly, trembling at the hand of some unknown entity much stronger than myself. I was alone in the living room, could hear the sounds of sleep coming from the open bedroom door. I dragged myself to the bathroom, the scent of copper thick in the back of my throat, sure that this was the end.

Esti found me in the morning, laying helplessly next to the proof of something gone horribly wrong, my neck too weak to balance the pounding in my head no matter how valiantly I tried to let them know that I was okay.

I was not okay.

They rushed me to the doctor, the light still a hazy beam on the horizon. I had no fight left in me that morning, waited patiently for my turn and let the doctors and nurses manipulate the shell of my body however they pleased. Cate held my head in the crook of her elbow and willed me to try while Esti did her best to field the doctor's questions through the hiccoughing staccato of her breaths.

"...hasn't been eating... only a couple of days... not normal for him, no... not even his favorite biscuits... still active, but slower..."

As she battled through the laundry list of warning signs, the doctor nodded solemnly, her eyes carefully sympathetic even while her hands gathered and adjusted and measured and soothed.

"...run some tests... probably a stroke... keep him here overnight...we'll call you if anything changes..."

It wasn't until later, after I'd been pinched and poked and prodded, laid flat on a cold slab of metal while a machine whirred noisily above me, and then tucked into a blanket as they did their rounds, that I realized I'd been abandoned.

I'd forgotten to worry about that, with all these years of creature comforts and familial bliss smoothing my once-rough edges.

They'd left me, after all.

Was this the last time? Would I ever see them again?

08/

The injections started soon after they brought me home from the hospital.

The first time Esti tried to inject me at home, she made the mistake of showing me the needle, that pointed arbiter of nausea and unease that had become a perpetual affront to my own agency.

Her second mistake was thinking she could inject me without a fight.

Oh, what a fight it was. Upended chairs and the rug in disarray, both of us wide-eyed and panting on opposite sides of the table, sweat beading on her brow, her determination an entity all its own.

I was impressed, but she would have to call in some backup if she wanted to get anywhere near me anytime soon. I wouldn't make it easy for her.

She called Cate in, the ultimate betrayal. They worked together, and their cohesiveness would have been spectacular if it hadn't been aggressively pointed in my direction. I fought, valiantly, but to no avail.

They injected me once a week for over a year.

I hated the way the medication made me feel, like I was dragging myself through quicksand threatening to take me down with a horrifying slurp of finality. It was always a relief when it wore off, giving me a few days respite before it dragged me down again. I never let on when its effects abated, not while they were watching, anyway, in case it made them forget.

I was never hungry when it took hold of me, and I took to hiding my food in the couch cushions and in the soil of the potted plants so they wouldn't be disappointed in me. I wanted to make them happy, and I still cared what they thought, but I wasn't prepared to give up my independence. The less they knew, the better.

We were all distraught when I kept losing weight and started turning yellow again, the sickly pallor contrasting with my black fur to create an effect not unlike a bumble bee.

"We need to go back to the hospital," I heard Esti whispering one night when they thought I wasn't listening. "He's getting worse. What else can we do?"

Loss of agency was slightly better than being stuck in the sterility of a hospital again, so I started forcing down enough food to ensure their attention would slip and I could go into the other room and sulk in peace.

It worked, for a time, but there were days when I couldn't convince my legs to carry me over to the table, knew what I was expected to do but couldn't bring myself to do it. They brought the food to me, spooned it into my mouth with kindness, gentle but firm. Against my will.

"You need fuel to fight. Please eat something."

Things got better when Cate realized I could stomach boiled chicken, could force it down my throat one bite at a time even on the worst of days. I felt bad, watching Esti slave over the stove early in the morning to make sure she had a fresh batch ready for me when it was breakfast time, but not bad enough to refuse it.

I was grateful, felt lucky to have people in my life who would go above and beyond without so much as an eye roll. I ate the chicken, and did my best to make them believe it was helping even when I didn't think that anything could.

09/

I refused to eat anything but chicken those last few years.

I didn't want the healthy slop Esti prepared for me, no matter how many times they tried to convince me that it was for my own good. I'd been on this earth long enough to know what I liked, and puréed vegetables weren't going to make the cut, vitamin content be damned.

I took my meals in front of my programs, always. I appreciated the brief respite of escapism, the background noise a balm to my battered body, the fleeting images of birds and squirrels a reminder of who I had been and what I had had.

We visited countless sterile doctor's offices during that period, which I made no secret of hating. I would kick and scream and complain the whole way there, loath to admit that their kindness, never ending as it was patient, was comforting.

I may have been loath to admit it, but I was grateful for it all the same.

What is it about age that makes us act out? Like we're testing the boundaries of everyone's patience, even our own. I thought I'd grown out of my rebellious streak. My younger self would never have put up with the me I'd become, but at least he wasn't around to see what a mess I'd made of things. How limited my capacity. How shrunken my kingdom.

I still took up space, but I knew I was hindering their movement. They left less, and never together, and in my most selfish moments I let myself believe it was because they preferred my company. I preferred theirs, after all, even when I shut myself away in the other room and lost myself to my dreams, though I never would have said it to them. We'd been together long enough for them to know my heart without needing to hear the words.

Cate recorded my favorite song for me one day, before she left on one of those long trips, and Esti would play it for me just before she'd turn off all the lights and head to bed. It was a small thing, but it helped keep the sadness at bay until the morning, when I knew we were one day closer to the day we'd all be back together.

I might have been grumpy more often than not, but together is all I ever really wanted to be.

10/

We didn't need to be told it was time.

From the moment I let out an anguished cry in the front hallway and collapsed into a puddle of my own vomit, the end had barreled toward us with alarming efficiency.

Esti rushed me to the emergency room, her soothing words belied by the set of her shoulders—strong and square and steadfast—and the forced smile that couldn't quite reach her eyes. We'd both known my time was coming to an end for some years by then, though we'd taken care to disguise our concerns from each other with our silly games and traditions.

There would be no more ignoring it now.

In truth, I'd be lying if I said it wasn't a relief. There are only so many pills and injections one can tolerate, but I would have sold my soul to rid her of the tears welling up in her eyes that she kept turning away to wipe so that I wouldn't worry.

The doctor was kind, as always. I'd met my fair share of medical professionals with chips on their shoulders, and had been grateful to find this one, with his kind eyes and gentle hands.

It didn't make a lick of difference in the end, though, how soft his words could be.

"It's time."

Esti shuddered, biting back a sob.

"Okay. I just need to make a phone call. Give us a few minutes, please."

She called Cate, gone on one of her long trips. I could hear the sleep in her voice when she wrestled herself out of sleep on the second ring.

"What happened? Is he okay?"

"It's time."

"Okay. Put me on video so I can see him."

I was too tired by then to understand the words, but I heard the emotion behind them, familiar, safe, all-encompassing, and very much like love.

"I love you, okay? I'm going to miss you so much, but it's okay to go now. I know you have to go. I love you."

There was so much I wanted to say, but neither the time nor the energy were within my control.

Cate had given in to the tears, then, her voice hoarse with loss and lack of sleep. She blinked at me, and I blinked back, and then the phone was pulled away and I heard the tinny whisper of their goodbyes in the background of the fluorescently lit room.

"One more thing, please."

She fumbled with her phone for a moment, and I gasped when I heard the first chords of my favorite song, the one Cate would always play for me that could put me to sleep no matter how stubbornly I clung to waking. I closed my eyes, Esti's hand soothing circles on my back while the strings rang out softly in stereo somewhere next to my head.

"It's okay to let go, now. It's time. We love you. Don't forget us...we'll never forget you."

I'd like to be going home today, but I don't think that's in the cards for me anymore. I'll be left behind this time, but I'll know it won't be because they didn't want me, or because we didn't try hard enough to stay together. Whatever doubts I may have at some time harbored about my place in life, I now knew without question that I belonged with them, always. That I was wanted. That I was loved.

And at least I had enough memories to surround me for whatever would come next.

I sighed, giving in to sleep for the last time.

One Big Do-Over

Kimberly Smith

I tap the quill onto a linen scrap and watch the midnight blot diffuse along the fibers. Ideas float off the threads, and my heroine continues her story...

She descended from the carriage, lifting the yellow, vermilion, and pale-blue silk robes to give her legs room to move. Zhu Huiyong—provincial princess, adventurer, spy—wound her way through the bazaar, scanning for today's contact. She would know him by his black cape—an odd thing to wear in midsummer in western Sichuan.

Would he be handsome or wrinkled? The message hidden within the veins of the fan left outside her chamber only told her to look for the black cape today, in this market. He would have information desired by the chief of guards. She hid a purse of local coin in an inside pocket.

The air swirled with hints of cinnamon, turmeric, roasting birds, and the rot of opium—reminders that she'd rather be at home, even as she expected some unknown danger to await her.

Her fine robes contrasted with the dull linens worn by dirt-besmirched, screeching street urchins and their unkempt parents. She reminded herself that as emissary—and daughter—of the Honorable Governor, she was meant to command respect. Aware of the villagers' stares, she straightened and lifted her chin. But could they see it quiver, or hear the heartbeat pounding in her ears? Would they doubt her as much as she doubted herself?

She reached inside the folds of her robe, confirming the purse was still there, and slowly exhaled a steadying breath. Where was her contact? Perhaps she needed to wait, buy mangoes, herbs, or a wobbly pot. She imagined spies behind every door— or Mongol horsemen thundering toward the village. Her legs shook even as she pretended to care about the vivid tents and hawking merchants.

Children darted past, nearly knocking her over. Barking dogs and a shouting vendor scrambled after them. She reached out to steady herself, grabbing a nearby cart loaded with orange turmeric root, dried herbs, and medicinal tinctures in wine and mead. She read labels that warned of toxins, hallucinogens, and purgatives. She gripped the cart—maybe there was something she could use, just in case.

Someone moved behind her—too close for comfort or propriety. She spun, seeing no one. A hand clamped over her mouth with a cloth soaked in an herbal concoction. She fought to twist free, but the hand held firm. She choked, clawed at the arm, felt coarse linen and rough hair. Panic rose. Not now, please, no. She tried to scream, but no sound came. Her knees buckled; she began to swoon. Colors blurred, sounds receded, and the world tilted. Reaching blindly for the apothecary's cart, she knocked it over, and its contents spilled over her.

Darkness won.

When she woke, her wrists were bound behind a pole, her silk replaced with scratchy sackcloth. Her head pounded. Her vision was fuzzy, mouth fuzzier. Her tongue traced a swollen lip and she could not open her right eye.

Kidnapped. Beaten? How had this happened? As a member of the royal family of Zhu, she should not have been manhandled. Panic started, but gave way to indignation as she gritted her teeth and growled.

Diffuse light filtered through the weave of the tent walls, illuminating trapped dust motes. All was in tones of red and brown—rugs, collapsible chairs, a folding table piled with baskets and scrolls. I have to escape. I must find a way. She imagined unweaving a basket to make a rope. Maybe a chair leg would do as a weapon. She tugged on the ties that trapped her arms, but the ties held tight.

* * *

I lift my quill as I lose the flow of ideas. I chew my bottom lip and stroke the side of the feather across my cheek.

I named my heroine Huiyong: Hui for bright and kind, and Yong for brave and fierce. She is clever, like me, but much braver. She will find a way to escape—but how? A striking stranger to the rescue? A clutched herbal tincture? Or will the Mongol horsemen overturn the tent in their attack? She certainly would not expect rescue from her father's guards.

I gaze satisfied at my scrolls, open around me on the library table. Adventures in distant lands dance in my twelve-year-old imagination.

The characters of my language form the shapes of the horse, the river, the moon over mountains. I love writing these stories, and I thrill at pretending a life outside these walls.

My father enters the room. I do not hear him until he slaps the quill from my hand, smearing the last few characters.

"MeLin, you are a princess, not a common secretary." His face is red, his jaw hard.

"But," I begin to complain as I right the spilled ink bottle with shaking hands, and bend to fetch the quill. "But—" I don't know how to explain to him what this means to me. I have a gift. It shouldn't be wasted. But he is so angry.

"No buts. Clean this up and hurry to tea ceremony training." He storms out.

I stare at the swirling cloud of dust in his wake, glowing in a beam of afternoon sun. The quill slips from my trembling fingers and softly pings as it hits the floor. It bounces then settles into a spreading blotch of indigo. I drop to my knees, fighting back tears.

I must honor my father. I must behave as a princess. I know from this moment I shall never write again. Lifting my chin, I swallow my tears, rip up the scrolls, and stomp on the stained feather.

I drag myself to the tea ceremony training.

Mrs. Li bows deeply as I settle onto the brocade cushion set out for me.

She drones on and on. "Produced in the Meng Mountains here in Sichuan... tribute to the Emperor... five elements represented in the art... grind into powder... whisking in a ceramic bowl..."

I imagine Huiyong on horseback with bales of freshly picked, aromatic tea leaves; a celadon-glazed pot wrapped in sheepskin, tucked safely into leather saddlebags. They ascend into the mountains toward the Imperial Palace to pay the tribute. The horse strains, his breath visible in the chill of high elevation. Shale crumbles beneath his hooves, clattering down the pass. Huiyong leans forward for balance. The horse whinnies and rears as a small band of armed smugglers surrounds her.

"MeLin." Mrs. Li slaps the bamboo whisk against my wrist.

I jerk, pull back my hands, and lower my eyes.

"You dishonor your father. Pay attention."

I grind the leaves into lumpy bits. My hands shake as I pour the boiling water. Droplets bloom across the silk table cover. Whisking sends more dark blobs spreading through the fabric. Acid rises in my throat.

Mrs. Li grunts. Through tight lips she spits, "You will never master this." She bows as she leaves—though she doesn't hold one bit of respect for me.

A tear slips down my cheek. She's right. I cannot master something that does not move my heart.

I pretend Huiyong bursts into the tea room on horseback, knocking over the ceremonial objects. She reaches a hand toward me and hoists me up behind her. I wrap my arms around her waist as we thunder away.

* * *

The years pass like paintings fading in the sun.

At sixteen, I marry the court treasurer. My father hopes his older, tedious administrator will make me more practical. Instead, I wander in the Governor's gardens, talking to plants and fish. My husband hires women to attend to the various household and personal needs. I want to have an audience with my father, to complain or ask for a divorce, but he has shut me out of his life.

At twenty-eight, both my father and husband are dead. I am a wealthy widow, but without heirs, business, or remarriage prospects. I wander the halls of my father's home, partly dressed. I watch the koi in the garden for hours, mumbling to them about far away lands. I have a vague memory of something I wanted to do, something...

For my fortieth birthday, Mrs. Li visits. A gray, bent, dowager, she convinces me to go on an excursion. I can see the pity in her eyes, but I agree. She helps me prepare for the Spring bazaar.

I descend from my carriage, lifting the yellow, vermilion, and pale-blue silk robes. The swirl of hues and scents triggers a memory—was it real, or one of my fantasies? Am I here to meet someone in a black cape? To find an apothecary's cart? A tent in reds and browns? My pulse quickens.

I meander through the marketplace, fingertips brushing smooth mangoes and rough stoneware rims. I spin as children dash past me, chased by an angry vendor. Everything feels slow and muffled, as if under water. *Huiyong—is that my name? Or am I called MeLin?*

I am drawn into a hut filled with smoke and a sickly-sweet aroma that clings to my throat. I take the seat prepared for me, pass a purse of coin, and accept the pipe. The edges of my world soften. Shapes and colors fold in on themselves in a whirlpool of images. For a few extended moments, I fly to the lands I always wanted to visit—on horseback, with dragons, fighting tyrants, being the heroine I longed to be, honored by my father, the Emperor.

The visions dissolve into white light. I ascend beyond the veil— before language, before longing. Only silence. Only release.

"Welcome home."

I recognize the voice of my guardian angel. All is softness here— the gentle light, quiet music, a hint of jasmine, the feeling of enveloping acceptance.

"Oh." Tears well up. "I didn't do what I meant to do." The tears fall. Sadness engulfs me.

My angel offers a silk tissue and strokes my back. "But it was quite an adventure, wasn't it?"

"I wish—" I sniffle. I sigh.

"What, Love?"

"I wish I could do it over, do it differently." I look deeply into her eyes, hoping, but not expecting, her to grant the wish.

She smiles and takes my hand. In a blink, we arrive in a quiet corner of my old library. I see myself at twelve, seated at the desk with scrolls, ink, and quill, feeling the joy of putting my stories on paper.

The angel nudges me gently.

As I merge into my younger body, she whispers, "Go ahead. Try again."

I feel the tightness of my body, gravity pulling me ever downward. I smell the ink, feel the paper and the quill. I stare at my fingers, wondering what I was doing.

My father steps in to the library, surprising me. He swats. He yells.

I see the anger in his face and my heart races. I stand and bow deeply. "Father," I clear my throat, my voice weak and crackly. "I ... I wish to honor you. I will hurry to my appointment, but—"

He grunts and turns toward the door.

I reach for his hand, trembling. "First—"

He stares, surprised at my ink-stained fingers against his white skin. I pull back and tuck my hands inside my robes.

"First, read this. It might—delight." The words tumble quickly into the charged air. I chew my bottom lip. My heart pounds with hope.

He squints. I nod and bow again.

He leans over and reads my story, reaching to touch the smeared characters. "What happens next?" he whispers.

I beam. *He likes it! He sees my talent.* After a steadying breath, I grin. "Tea ceremony."

The right side of his mouth twitches. He nods ever so slightly. "Be quick."

* * *

At sixteen, I am walking the garden paths, humming to myself, when the mounted Captain of the Guard surprises me.

He bows from his saddle. "Princess."

"Captain." I bow back and reach to scratch the patch of white on the horse's forehead. "What is her name?" I stroke gently.

"Meng."

"Like the mountains where so much tea is grown?" I know the history and artistry of the tea ceremony. It is one of my favorite practices, second only to writing.

"Yes, Princess."

I peer at the Captain around Meng's short mane. He is perhaps thirty, muscular, sun-darkened from his station outdoors. A thin diagonal scar mars his chin. *Is he married?*

"If it is not too forward of me... what is your name?"

"Zuan Han, Princess." He tilts his head.

"Han, like the poet, Wang Han?" I have read Wang Han in *Three Hundred Tang Poems. Is this soldier a poet too?* My heart skips a beat.

"Yes, Princess." Is that a blush brushing his cheeks?

"Well, Zuan Han, I am a writer. I invent adventure stories—with horses and travel and a handsome consort." Now I'm the one blushing. I breathe deeply for courage. Huiyong would ask without hesitation, so I take the chance. "I am practicing the tea ceremony. Would you do me the honor of attending? I'm still quite clumsy and need the practice. You would truly be assisting me." I hold my breath waiting, hoping.

It takes several eternal moments before he replies. "Yes, Princess." He bows deeply.

My father objects for several months to our marriage. "I forbid it. He's a commoner."

I counter, "He's honorable," or "He's strong and protective," or "He loves me."

Eventually Father relents as he sees how I become like whirling autumn leaves when Han is near.

For our honeymoon, we travel along the Great Wall for six month. It is glorious. I have to purchase more scrolls and ink to keep up with the flourishing story ideas.

We stop in Nanjing on our way to greet the Emperor. I visit printer after printer, trying to have my manuscripts published, but they take one look at me and decline. "You are a child," or "You are no scholar," or "You are a woman." I slam the door of the last printer behind me.

Han reassures me. "Maybe in Sichuan." He lifts me, sets me gently into our carriage, and steals a long, hungry kiss.

I try but cannot hide my heartbreak. My writing suffers. I miscarry on the way home. My writing stops entirely. I tear up the latest impossible story—and the dark one before it.

A year passes in quiet. I ignore my dreams. I decline visits. A caravan bound for Constantinople stops in my village and leaves without me.

After our son, Han, is born, I read poetry to him to help him sleep. His father brings out some of my old scrolls and encourages me to read the stories aloud. I am reluctant at first, but the child lights up, smiles, and giggles as I act out the scenes. His first word, after *papa* and *mama*, sounds slightly like "Huiyong." Perhaps I imagine it, but it is enough to make me revisit my stories with wiser eyes.

Han takes three of my rewritten stories to a printer, and they are published with the author's name: Zuan Wenhan, first son of Zuan Han. I whine but see no other option.

When the printer asks for more manuscripts, I—like Huiyong—insist they are published under my own name. I imagine my soldier husband standing tall before the shriveled printer, demanding my due. Next time, *I* visit the printer. *I* make the arrangements.

At twenty-eight, my heart breaks twice: I send ten-year old Han to boarding school a week after my father dies. I write furiously about grief and emptiness until I have emptied myself of both. No words, no stories touch the void.

I sit by the koi pond for hours, speaking to the fish about my appreciation of my father and my hopes for my son and the loss of my courageous heroine.

"Princess?" Han approaches me on his new steed, Yin Ying—Shadow.

I smile, remembering our first meeting. "Yes, Captain?" I reach up to scratch Yin Ying's forehead. My silver-haired husband is still fit in uniform, though lines crease his eyes and mouth. The scar on his chin has deepened.

"There's a caravan heading to Siberia. I'm to go as an envoy. Would you like to accompany me?" His eyes twinkle. He knows my longing to travel.

"Oh, I don't know," I tease. "I have a great many things to do here."

"If I let you bring your scrolls and ink?"

"If you let me? What?" I feign indignation, though excitement bubbles up from my toes. I chew my bottom lip, considering. "How soon?"

At forty, I bury my husband. Life stops for a while. Our son is studying with an apothecary and cannot come home for months.

Mrs. Li, my former tea ceremony teacher, visits after the mourning period. Her shaking hand grips my forearm. "Let me take you on a small adventure, to honor Han." Even bent nearly double, she still commands me.

We arrive at the bazaar I have described in so many stories. Lifting my yellow, vermillion, and pale blue silk robes, I descend from the carriage. She hobbles beside me as I glide through the aisles between tents.

People greet me with warm smiles. I buy an aromatic meal of roasted bird and root vegetables stewed with tea leaves. My coachman delivers some of my scrolls to a merchant. Children gather as I read from my latest adventure. They applaud as the heroine vanquishes the enemy and kisses her consort.

As the crowd thins, I notice a middle-aged woman in servant's garb lingering beside the tent. A frayed, carefully folded scroll trembles between her wringing hands. I bow to her—appropriate to our stations. "May I help you?"

She bows deeply. "I wished to thank you, Princess. Your story, the one where Huiyong tricked a kidnapper and escaped violence—my daughter did the same to her employer. She lost her position, but not her virtue."

My mouth falls open. No words come. My father's phrase, "common secretary," echoes in my mind, and dissipates.

Mrs. Li squeezes my arm. "See? Your stories are not merely entertainment."

* * *

Decades later, a paper booklet falls from my hands as I leave my body.

"Welcome back." My guardian angel wraps me in her sweet embrace. I surrender into her warmth, releasing the ache of lifetimes into her arms. In moments, I expand into the freedom of my light body. I breathe deeply into the world of spirit and feel love and joy rise from my core.

"I did it. I did what I wanted to do." I raise my arms in victory and glow with pleasure.

My angel grins broadly and waves her wings in celebration.

After a rest, we settle into the softest of theater chairs for my life review. Scenes unfold on dual screens, a different timeline on each.

I sigh, watching on one screen as I retreat further into myself. The household servants are moved to care more for their own loved ones. I see my father withering like grapes left untended on the vine. On the other, I observe my dark and sad times and how I returned to courage—returned to writing. I witness the impact of my kindness on a fellow traveler in Siberia, who went on to save a tiger and her cubs.

I whisper, "Just because of a few words?"

I smile as I watch a young girl stand up to an abusive brother after she saw me confront a swindler on a caravan. I press my hand to my heart, seeing readers in dark moments glimpse hope in my stories and find the will to live again.

"I had no idea."

My angel squeezes my shoulders.

On the screen I see my father beaming with pride, even though he would never show it to me in person. I sniffle and wipe my eyes with the back of my hand. "Both lives feel so vital. Which one was real?"

Her presence shines brighter. "Both were real. Both were lived. Both brought gifts to your soul."

A circle of ancestors gathers around us, reaching forward to touch my shoulders. Father, Mother, grandparents, and deep into history—I melt into their love and approval, tilting my head onto my father's hand.

The angel pauses a moment, cherishing the beings around us. She nods to Father and he lingers near, his part of my life review not yet complete. As the other spirits recede, she turns back to the screens. They zoom in on moments when I was twelve and interrupted by my father—the quill that fell, the scrolls I ripped up with trembling hands, and the long quiet life afterward. Then, the other timeline, where I reached out, trembling, inviting understanding, and picked up the quill again.

"I see." I whisper, strength expanding my heart. "It was my choice to turn away, replaying the rejection in my mind. I forbade myself from writing stories. It was also my choice to reach out, invite my father into my world, risking further rejection." The two sets of emotion swirl within me and I settle more deeply into the soft seat with a deep sigh.

"And?" She raises one eyebrow.

I watch more scenes of my father, his feeling lost with my withdrawal; lifted with my success. "Oh, he needed *me* to be creative for *his* soul's growth."

She nods and beams at my father, inviting him nearer.

He takes my hands. "MeLin, you helped free me." He looks deeply into my eyes. "And, please forgive me."

Tears slide down my cheeks. "Of course. I understand. And you helped free me—you, and my fantasy heroine who gave me courage to try again and again."

The angel turns to me. "What do you desire next?"

"To continue creating. Yes. That is fun and fulfilling; it is brave— and it matters."

Han steps forward from the mists and takes my hand. For us, a peaceful rest—how long, I cannot say.

* * *

Somewhere on Earth, in another century, a young girl dips her fountain pen into an inkwell and stares at the crackling fireplace. She chews her bottom lip. Sparks float up the chimney as the aroma of pine fills the room.

With a vague sense of déjà vu, a satisfied smile spreads across her face as she turns to her paper. She scratches out:

Poetry Assignment
There once was a princess of China
Whose clothes could not have been finer.
She went to the market
To buy a gold locket
But then Mongol thieves gagged and tied her.
She giggles. *Well, it's a start.*

Kill Two Birds

Susan Brearley

One—The Drive

The clean laundry went in last, after the body.

I merged onto Route 47. Forty-two in a forty-five zone. Just another driver heading home from her Saturday night laundry run at the Riverside Airbnb. The route I'd memorized down to every pothole since taking on the Riverside property.

Predictable. That's what he'd counted on.

My knitting bag had overturned in the struggle, sending yarn across the floor mat. Alpaca blend, lovely stuff, sixty dollars a skein. Worth more than the man in my trunk, depending on who you ask. The bamboo needles were back in the door pocket where they belonged. Size 10, perfect for chunky scarves and other quick projects.

He'd been waiting in that dark space behind the driver's seat, pressed against the floor. Patient. I had to admire the commitment. Must have slipped in while I was loading the washer. Tucked himself behind me like a shadow, waiting for me to buckle in. To trap myself for him.

In my books, fight scenes run for pages of choreographed violence. In real life, three minutes change everything. He'd known my name before I killed him. "Carol," he said urgently.

"The baby shoes, Carol. Still tied together. Nobody reported how the laces were knotted. How did you know how they were tied?"

The rest of whatever he'd planned to say was currently mixing with industrial-strength Tide and whatever else leaked out of fresh trauma. I'd written about it dozens of times. The body's immediate betrayals. Funny how different it smells in real life.

Less copper, more iron. Or maybe that was the blood on my good cardigan.

There was a deer up ahead, a skinny thing, just standing there on the shoulder. She just stared at me, then bolted.

Smart creature. I kept driving.

Mile marker 23. Maria would ordinarily clean the Riverside property tomorrow at noon. I'd text her in the morning that I'd already stripped the beds and done the towels. "Thought I'd help out since I was doing my own laundry anyway. Kill two birds with one stone!"

Kill two birds. Christ. The phrases we use.

His driver's license was in my purse. Ryan M— something. I'd seen the first name when I grabbed it and stopped there. Ryan was enough. Ryan, who noticed the knots. The man who thought I'd witnessed something. Written about something real.

Or maybe I had.

The notebook in my pocket felt heavier than the body in the trunk. Spiral-bound, the kind reporters used to carry. I had pulled it from his jacket when I was checking his pockets, a quick rifle through his pockets, looking for practical things. His keys had been in his jacket pocket—a Subaru fob, newish. He'd probably parked at the trailhead near the Riverside property, where hikers left cars overnight all the time. It would be days before anyone noticed.

But my fingers had brushed pages covered in my own words. Highlighted passages. Dates in the margins.

I'd read exactly one line before stopping: "Page 47, paragraph 3, impossible she could know unless..."

Unless what, Ryan something?

There was a rest stop at mile marker 31. Good lighting, security cameras, and busy enough that one more traveler using the facilities wouldn't register. They had those metal drums for cigarette disposal. Amazing how hot those things burned when you fed them enough paper.

The notebook would disappear there. Whatever conspiracy he'd mapped out between my fiction and someone's reality would become ash and drift. I'd never know what he thought I knew. Never find out if he was crazy or if I'd accidentally stumbled onto something true.

My phone buzzed. Text from my daughter: "Still doing laundry this late? You work too hard, Mom."

I voice-texted back: "Just finished. Home soon. Love you."

Normal. Except for the man who'd known about the baby shoes, currently marinating in industrial-strength Tide. I'd written a scene like this once—amateur killer thinks detergent destroys DNA. It doesn't. But I wasn't trying to hide evidence.

I just really hated blood on my clean laundry.

Two—38 Minutes Earlier

Eleven-seventeen, and nobody should be here but me.

I was folding pillowcases. The 800-thread-count Egyptian cotton that guests paid $200 a night to sleep on. My knitting bag sat by the front door, bamboo needles tucked in the side pocket where I always kept them. I'd been working on a scarf during the spin cycle—alpaca blend, a Christmas gift for my daughter. The kind of grandmother thing I did because I was that lady who owned rental properties and wrote mysteries and sometimes did laundry at eleven o'clock on a Saturday night.

The motion sensor light didn't trigger.

The light should have caught any movement on the driveway. Should have flooded the front yard with those harsh LEDs that made everything look like a crime scene.

It didn't.

I set down the pillowcase. Moved to the window. My Camry was parked right outside, trunk open, waiting for the clean laundry. The interior light was on—I'd left the driver's door ajar, just planning to load up and go.

No light on the driveway. No movement in the yard.

But someone had been here. Was here. I could feel it the way you feel someone watching you in a crowded room.

I grabbed my phone. My keys. The laundry basket with the whites. Typical movements. Just another housekeeper, finishing up, heading home. If someone was watching—and someone was—they'd see exactly what they expected to see.

I shouldered the front door open. Thirty feet to my car. The gravel crunched under my shoes—comfy Dansko clogs, practical, good arch support. The kind of detail I'd use in a book. The kind of detail that makes a character real.

The November air bit at my throat. Clear night. Half moon. Enough light to see the tree line, the shapes of the pines against the sky.

Not enough light to see him.

I loaded the basket into the trunk. Slid it in next to the detergent bottles and the fabric softener. Closed the trunk with that solid Toyota thunk—the Camry was fifteen years old but built well.

I opened the driver's door. Slid in. Reached for my seatbelt.

That's when I felt the air change.

Not movement. Not sound. Just the sense of occupied space behind me.

In every one of my mysteries, the protagonist reaches for a gun, or their phone, or a panic button.

Muscle memory can save your life.

Here, in real life, I reached for my seatbelt to hightail it out of there.

It was dark. I told myself, you are being ridiculous.

The wire came over my head before I finished the thought.

It bit in. Metal. Thin. Professional.

My hands went to my throat. Pure animal instinct. Fingers scrabbling for the wire, trying to get underneath it, pull it away from the windpipe. Useless. He was pulling from behind, using the headrest for leverage. Every time I pulled forward, he pulled harder.

I couldn't breathe.

Not couldn't get a full breath—couldn't—breathe. Nothing. The wire had closed my airway completely.

Three minutes. I'd written this in Chapter 8 of The Riverside Killer. Three minutes without oxygen and brain cells start dying. Permanent damage. After six minutes, you're gone, even if someone revives the heart.

I was maybe fifteen seconds in and already the edges of my vision were going gray.

He said something. I couldn't hear over the roaring in my ears—the sound of blood trying to reach my brain through a closing passage. Later, I'd be haunted by how he uttered my name. Like a personal, desperate plea.

My left hand was still at my throat. Still pulling uselessly at the wire.

My right hand dropped.

Not a conscious decision. Not tactical thinking. Just the blind animal part of my brain that wasn't oxygen-starved yet, the part that said do—something—do—anything—don't—die—don't—die—don't die—

The door pocket.

The bamboo needles were always there. Size 10, chunky gauge. I'd been using them for years. Knew the weight of them, the heft, the way the bamboo had a slight flex that kept them from being brittle.

My fingers closed around one.

I didn't think. Couldn't think. Just drove it backward over my shoulder with everything I had.

The resistance of the fabric first. Then skin. Then something deeper—muscle, maybe, or fat, I didn't know or care. The needle bent but didn't break. Bamboo does that. Flexes instead of snapping.

He screamed.

The wire went slack.

I could breathe.

That first gasp was fire down my throat. The sweetest, most agonizing thing I'd ever felt. I threw myself against the driver's door, hands scrabbling for the handle, got it open, half-fell out of the car onto the gravel.

Turned.

Saw him.

He was in the back seat, one hand to his face. Blood between his fingers. The needle was still there, buried in his cheek just below the left eye. Size 10 bamboo, twelve inches long, with about four inches protruding from his face.

He was making sounds. Not words. Just sounds.

I should have run.

That's what my protagonist would do. Get distance. Get help. Call 911 and let the professionals handle it.

Instead, I reached back into the car. There were more needles in the car door pocket. He saw me reach for another one. He tried to talk, "Wait, Carol—" I aimed.

The second needle was in my hand. He saw it. Tried to lunge forward, away from me, but he was wedged in the back seat, tangled in his own jacket. The first needle still jutted from his cheek, moving when his face moved, and I saw him try not to scream every time it shifted.

He got his feet under him. Tried to climb over the center console, get to the front seat, and get away. But I was already pulling the back door open.

He saw my focus and said, "wait—Carol—I'm not—"

I grabbed his jacket. He was heavier than I expected, or I was weaker, or both. He tried to twist away, but the jacket gave me leverage.

The needle in my right hand was just a tool. Just a thing. I drove it toward him.

He caught my wrist.

His hand was huge next to my delicate forearm, and we were frozen in time for just an instant, him half out of the car, me pulling him, both of us grappling at the needle like it was a kid's game of tug-of-war.

But this was a squid game.

"I'm not here to hurt you," which was the most preposterous pleading I'd ever heard given the last few minutes. Blood covered his teeth, making him look like a Halloween creature. The needle in his face wobbled. "I just have a question—"

I twisted my wrist. Tried to break his grip. Couldn't.

So I kicked him.

My hard-soled Dansko connected with his shin, and I heard the crack. He grunted, and his grip loosened just enough for me to wrench my arm free and swing.

Not a stab. A swing. Like I was swatting a fly.

The needle caught him on the side of his head.

Not through the ear. Near it. The needle scraped along his skull, bent, then found the soft space just behind his ear where the bone curves inward.

And sank.

He made a sound. Not a scream. Something higher, thinner. His eyes went wide.

I let go of the needle. Stepped back.

He was half-in, half-out of the car, one leg still on the back seat. Both hands went to his head. To the needle. He was trying to pull it out but his fingers kept slipping on the bamboo, slick with blood now.

"Carol," he said. His voice sounded wrong. Slurred. "Carol, I—"

He fell.

Like a puppet in a show and someone just cut all his strings. He dropped to his knees on the gravel beside the car. His hands were clutching at his head, and then he fell onto his side, curling like one of those armadillo bugs.

His legs kicked. Once. Twice. Not purposeful movement. Just nerves firing, muscles spasming. I'd seen that before too. The last twitch of a swatted wasp.

I stood there.

In my books, I'd written scenes like this. That moment after violence. The world goes silent, but the killer's head is throbbing.

I'd always thought I'd gotten it right.

I had not.

There is an intensity in all your senses as the smells filter into the silence. A small breeze feels like a wind. A car sound in the distance sounds like it's right next door. All your senses are insanely heightened. You feel the gravity of your being alive, as you look at the leaking blood. You feel like one of the animals in the forest, the ones you watch from the safety behind the glass of your kitchen window.

He was still breathing. I could see his chest move. Shallow, fast breaths like a dog panting.

His eyes were open. Looking at nothing.

I should call 911. That's what you do. Even if you've killed someone in self-defense, you call. You get help. You let the system work.

I pulled my phone from my pocket.

Looked at the screen. Looked at him.

He'd been in my car. Hiding. Waiting. He'd tried to strangle me with a wire.

But he'd also said my name like he knew me. Said he had questions. Said he wasn't there to hurt me.

Maybe he was lying. Maybe he was telling the truth.

I'd never know now.

I put my phone away.

His breathing was slowing. The kicks had stopped. He just lay there on the gravel, curled on his side, the two needles jutting from him like bizarre acupuncture.

It took six minutes.

I'd written it wrong in Chapter 8. I'd said three minutes without oxygen causes brain death. But this was different. This was a penetrating brain injury. Brainstem, probably. The breathing center shutting down, slowly, while I watched.

At minute four, he tried to say something. Just a wet sound in his throat.

At minute five, his breathing stopped.

At minute six, I checked his pulse.

Nothing.

I stood up. Looked at my hands. No blood. How was there no blood on my hands?

The laundry basket was still in the trunk. The whites. The towels. The 800-thread-count pillowcases.

All clean.

I looked at this dead man who had known about a pair of baby shoes—a detail in one of my stories.

Then I looked at the trunk.

Three—Rest Stop

The body shifted going around the curve just before mile marker 28.

Just like the thumping blankets in the dryer, when they get all balled up.

That's what I told myself it sounded like.

I wasn't shaking. My hands were steady and firmly grasped the steering wheel.

I remembered writing about killers with shaking hands. It was a trope after every scene—the trembling fingers, the post-traumatic shock and awareness, the characters falling apart after the violent scenes.

None of that happened to me.

My hands were steady.

The rest stop was three miles after the curve. I knew this road by heart. Didn't even have to think about where the car seemed to know to go. Just like a horse on a well worn riding trail.

This station was clean and well-lit. There were security cameras all over. It felt safe. Even late at night.

I pulled into a spot away from the entrance. Turned off the engine.

The cigarette disposal bin was right there, twenty feet from my car. Tall metal cylinder, perpetually smoldering. I'd written a scene in Chapter 14 of The Vanishing Hour. Ashes flying out of a burn bin, forever lost evidence, now seeding thunder clouds.

The notebook was in my jacket pocket. Still there. Still heavy.

I could end this right now. Whatever Ryan had discovered, whatever conspiracy he'd mapped between my fiction and someone's reality—it could all disappear in smoke.

I opened my car door.

That's when the state police cruiser pulled in beside me.

My heart stopped.

Not metaphorically. An actual full body slam of the ventricle that had been floppy and loud my entire life. Always acted up when I got stressed.

The trooper got out. Not in a hurry. Just tired, end of shift, stopping for coffee. He didn't look at me. Didn't register my existence. Just headed for the convenience store entrance.

I should stay in the car. Lock the doors. Wait for him to leave.

Instead, I got out.

The notebook seared like a steak in my pocket. I could feel the cooling heat of that body in my trunk from here. Surely he could smell it. Surely he could hear my heart trying to escape my chest.

He held the door for me.

"Evening," he said.

"Thank you," I said. Then, because my mouth has never understood the concept of stopping: "Or I guess it's technically night now, isn't it? After midnight? Though I never know when evening officially ends. Is it midnight? Or is it whenever the sun goes down? I've always wondered about that."

He politely smiled and tipped his hat. The way people do when they are engaging out of an obligation.

"Late for you to be out," he said.

And there it was. The question. The interest. The beginning of something that could unravel everything.

I should say something brief. Something ordinary. "Just heading home. Have a good night, officer."

Instead, I said, "Oh, I own a rental property up near Pine Grove—Airbnb, you know how that is—and I do the laundry myself because the cleaners charge extra for linens, which seems ridiculous because isn't washing linens part of cleaning? But anyway, I was up there doing the towels and sheets and I got a late start because I was working on my book—I'm a writer, mysteries mostly, nothing you've heard of I'm sure, nobody has—and then I realized I hadn't eaten dinner so I had some crackers in the car, the whole wheat ones from Costco, do you shop at Costco? The one in Poughkeepsie is good but the parking lot is a nightmare on weekends—"

His smile had frozen. That polite-but-trapped expression I'd seen on my children's faces a thousand times. My daughter's voice in my head, *Why, Mom? Why do you do this?*

"—and so by the time I got the laundry done it was late, but I'm a night owl anyway, always have been, even as a child I was the baby who wouldn't sleep, drove my mother absolutely crazy, she used to say I was making up for all the sleep I'd get when I was dead, which is morbid when you think about it—"

"Well," he said, backing away toward the coffee station. "Drive safe."

"You too! I mean, stay safe. Since you're working. Thank you for your service!" I gave him a little wave.

He fled.

I've never seen a cop do that before, unless they were getting a dispatch call.

He practically speed-walked to the furthest coffee dispenser from where I stood.

I was three feet away from the bored counter clerk who was busy scrolling his phone. The trooper was looking at coffee creamers like they held the answers to why his marriage was troubled.

The notebook was still in my pocket.

The cigarette bin was right outside.

But the trooper was here. Would be here for at least another five minutes. Getting coffee, maybe a sandwich, using the restroom. And those security cameras covered every angle of those bins.

I couldn't do it. Not now. Not with him here.

I bought a bottle of water I didn't want. Smiled at the clerk. Thanked him three times (because apparently I couldn't stop).

Walked back to my car.

The trooper was still inside. I could see him through the window, paying for his coffee, carefully not looking in my direction.

I got in my car. Started the engine. Put it in reverse.

Just a chatty lady who talks too much, heading home after doing laundry too late on a Saturday night.

The notebook stayed in my pocket.

Ryan stayed in my trunk.

And I drove home.

Four—Sunday Dinner

I got home around 1 AM. The driveway was empty—my daughter wouldn't arrive until tomorrow afternoon, four o'clock as always, prompt as sunrise.

The notebook sat on my kitchen table. I'd carried it inside first, before dealing with the trunk. Priorities.

I made tea. Earl Grey, Harney's, the good stuff. Sat down.

Opened the notebook.

Ryan's handwriting was meticulous. Engineer's hand, all caps, perfectly spaced. He'd marked up three of my stories with different colored highlighters. Yellow for details. Pink for dates. Green for what he called "impossible knowledge."

Page after page of my own words, reflected back at me through his obsession.

The baby shoes appeared on page 47 of "The Riverside Killer"—my second-best story, published in *Mystery Monthly* three years ago. I'd described them as "tiny white sneakers with blue laces, still tied together, the left shoe's lace knotted in a figure-eight at the base."

I'd made that up about the knot. Seemed like the kind of specific detail that made fiction feel real.

Except Ryan had written in the margin: "Figure-eight at the base. Exactly as I tied them. I never told anyone. How does she know?"

I turned the page.

More notes. More highlighting. A timeline he'd constructed, matching my publication dates against the baby shoes case. Poughkeepsie, 2019. Infant girl, six months old, found in a storage unit. Cause of death: blunt force trauma. Shoes still on her feet, tied together with a figure-eight knot.

The case went cold. No suspects. No arrests.

Ryan had written his confession on the last page. Not framed as confession—framed as terror. "She knows. Somehow she knows what only I could know. Following her Saturday schedule. Will confront at Riverside property. Need to understand HOW."

I closed the notebook.

Made more tea.

Sat there until the sky started turning that pre-dawn gray that meant I needed to get to work.

The thing about living alone on three acres backed by conservation land: you can do almost anything in your garage and nobody's around to hear it.

I'd butchered deer before. Helped my father dress game as a child. It's not so different with practice, and I'd written enough crime scenes to know the theory.

Theory, it turns out, is pretty close to practice.

By 9 AM, I had the meat grinder running. By 10, the first packages were wrapped and ready for the freezer. By noon, I had dealt with all the practical matters. The garage pickup had been useful. The conservation land, even more so.

By 11, I was walking into the tree line with a Costco bag of scraps.

The property line was two hundred feet back, where my lawn gave way to state forest. I scattered the first batch there, under the pines where the ground was soft with needles. Came back for another bag. Then another.

Deer hunters did this all the time—left gut piles for scavengers. Nature's cleanup crew. Circle of life and all that.

I was on my fourth trip when I heard the crows. They'd found it already. Smart birds.

At noon, I put a chicken in the oven—a real chicken, organic, from the co-op—and started on the potatoes. Sunday dinner with my daughter was sacred. Had been since she was small.

My phone rang at 12:30.

"Hey Mom, just wanted to confirm—four o'clock still good?"

"Perfect," I said, peeling carrots at the sink. Through the window, I could see two turkey vultures circling over the tree line. "I'm just doing dinner prep now."

"You're always cooking. Don't you ever rest?"

"I'll rest when I'm dead," I said. Then, because the universe has a sense of humor: "I'm making that roast chicken you like."

"The one with the rosemary?"

"That's the one."

"Perfect. Love you, Mom."

"Love you too, sweetheart."

I hung up. Went back to my carrots. The vultures were dropping lower now, spiraling down into the pines.

By 1 PM, I had the notebook burning in my fireplace. It went up fast—cheap paper, dry as kindling. I watched the pages curl and blacken, Ryan's meticulous notes becoming smoke, becoming nothing.

The baby shoes mystery would stay unsolved. Ryan would stay missing. And I would stay right here, cooking Sunday dinners and writing mysteries and scattering evidence where the coyotes could find it.

My daughter arrived at 4:03, apologizing for being late. Traffic on Route 47, always something.

We ate at the kitchen table, the good china, cloth napkins. She told me about work, about her kids, about the book she was reading. I told her about the Riverside property, about my latest story submission, about how I'd seen the most incredible wildlife lately.

"Really? Like what?"

"Turkey vultures this morning. Red-tailed hawk earlier—gorgeous bird. And there's a fox, beautiful red coat, probably has a den nearby. The Airbnb guests love spotting it."

She looked out the window at the tree line. A vulture was riding the thermals in the distance, dark wings spread wide.

"It's like living in a nature documentary back here."

"It really is," I said. "During the day, anyway. The fishers come out at night."

"Fishers?"

"Like a big weasel. Vicious things. They scream—sounds exactly like someone being murdered in the woods." I took a sip of water. "Terrifying if you don't know what it is."

"God, Mom. And you live out here alone."

"I like it," I said. "Keeps things interesting."

She took another bite of the roasted meat. Paused. "This is incredible, by the way. What did you do differently?"

"Nothing special. Just took my time with it. Low and slow, you know? Good things can't be rushed."

After she left—hugs, promises to call more often, the usual—I cleaned up. Washed the dishes. Put away the leftovers.

Sat down at my desk with my laptop.

I was 67 years old. Had maybe twenty good years left, if I was lucky. Fifteen if I was realistic. The heart arrhythmia wasn't getting better, and my mother had died at 72.

That was fifteen years to write. Fifteen years to finish the stories that were piling up in my head, demanding to be told.

I could spend them in a courtroom, explaining to twelve strangers that I'd killed a man in self-defense. That I'd panicked. That I'd made mistakes. That I was sorry.

Or I could spend them here. At this desk. Turning trauma into fiction, violence into narrative, truth into something close enough to be dangerous.

Ryan had been right about one thing: sometimes writers know things we shouldn't. Sometimes we write the confession before we know there's something to confess.

The screaming started just after midnight.

I was at my desk, three thousand words into a new story, when I heard it through my office window. That high, shrieking wail that sounds exactly like a woman being murdered in the forest.

The fishers had found my offering. Or maybe foxes—something was screaming out there in the dark.

I got up. Made more tea. Stood at the kitchen window and looked out at the black tree line.

I went back to my desk. My fingers hovered over the keys, then began typing.

"The wedding ring was still in the freezer, wrapped in aluminum foil, behind the lamb chops Patricia had been saving for Easter."

I stopped. Read it back.

Patricia. Where had that name come from? I didn't know anyone named Patricia.

But I somehow knew that the ring was white gold. Size 5.5. Patricia checked it every morning, moving the lamb chops aside with a single finger to ensure it was still there.

My fingers kept moving. "She'd killed him on garbage day. The trucks came early, before the neighbors woke."

The words poured out like truth from somewhere I'd never been.

Somewhere, maybe, a woman named Patricia was checking her freezer.

Somewhere, investigators might be looking for a ring.

Outside, the screaming continued.

I kept typing.

Contributors

Andrew DiMeo is a writer and mentor whose work bridges personal narrative, creative coaching, medical innovation, and whole-mind thinking. His education journey spans physics, English, secondary education, design, and a Ph.D. with a focus on biomedical engineering. He advises early-stage inventors through NIH and DARPA initiatives and builds projects where storytelling meets human potential. Away from work, he enjoys concerts, yoga, long bicycle rides, Airstream travel, and unhurried meals with loved ones.

Elle Fredine has been writing since Moses was in short pants, honing her craft online since 2008. Her work has been included in several print anthologies and featured in online publications. An accomplished artist, poet, and educator, she has spent thirty-plus years directing and designing for the theatre, and currently edits for five online publications. Writing as A.L. Fredine, she recently published an anthology of short stories and is working on two romance-mystery novels, one contemporary, one Edwardian.

Pascal Gambardella writes about his adventures in exploring the dynamics of human behavior. With a PhD in physics, he started his career as a mathematical physicist and later integrated psychology into his work. His popular works include poetry, satire, and articles on health, exercise, and mindful aging. His research now involves modeling the Classic Maya Collapse. He teaches Taekwondo and is a licensed life coach and Neuro-Semantics trainer.

Kathy Minicozzi is a retired opera singer. She has sung both concerts and leading roles in operas all over the world. She is now a solo cantor for St. John-Visitation Catholic Church in The Bronx, New York City. She has taken up a writing career, where she has written for Medium.com, Substack.com, and *Italian America Magazine*, as well as the Humor Outcasts website.

Stefanie Morejon is a writer, designer, teacher, linguist, and enthusiastic serial hobbyist from Miami, Florida. She currently lives in the Czech Republic with her partner and two questionably-behaved cats, scribbling down lines of inspiration on errant cocktail napkins, crumpled receipts, and the back of her hand. She dabbles in poetry and fiction, but believes the greatest stories are those that sneak up on us while we're busy living them.

Harrison Prisbrey is a poet, writer, and musician born and raised in Colorado. In his debut poem "Rest Well, Dear One" he draws upon his personal experience with meditation, rest, and the challenge of letting go to lead the reader through their own journey. Although this is his publishing debut, his poem "Tell Me" will be featured in the upcoming 2026 release of the anthology *Unhoused—Yearning for Home* by Prolific Pulse Press.

Erica Rose Shannon is a practicing Zen Buddhist who blends mindfulness practice with daily writing practice. She holds a Bachelor's degree in professional writing with a minor in communication and has been writing daily for over a decade. Known as Bold Truth Mama, Erica teaches writers to fearlessly speak their truth even when their voice shakes.

Kimberly Smith is a retired IT analyst and project manager, but that's only the facade. For decades, she has been exploring the spiritual, possibly non-ordinary world. Shamanism, herbalism, animism, healing, sacred ceremony, spirit-talking, ancestor rituals, and other weird things have taken hold of her imagination. Her writing dives into the deeper connection we all have with the spirits of love and healing, whether we acknowledge them or not.

Stephanie Wilson is a neurodiversity coach living in Virginia who writes mornings, afternoons, evenings—depending. She and her husband raised two sons, and now they're getting old—all of them. She used to run farther than you think is sane. She used to knit more than she should have but gave that up to draw cartoons. She holds an MFA and a neurodiversity coaching certification. She has no complaints, or not today.

Editor

Susan Brearley is a writer, editor, and teacher based in New York's Hudson Valley. She is the founder of the Garden of Neuro Institute, where she leads the Write Like Stephen King workshop and the Wordsmiths' Weekly writing community. Her work has appeared in *Chronogram* and across numerous publications on Medium, where she is EIC for 12 publications and a Top Writer in more than twenty categories. She is the author of *Battlefield Hope* and *Wordsmiths' Weekly Writing Prompts,* and a contributor to *The Talk, Safe and Brave Space, Fine Lines* and *I Am From* anthologies. *Emergent* grew from her belief that every writer deserves a seat at the table—and a reader who takes them seriously.

EMERGENT

About This Edition

This first edition of *Emergent: An Anthology of New Voices* was published
in December 2025 by Garden of Neuro Institute Publishing.

The text is set in Garamond, a typeface named for the
sixteenth-century Parisian engraver Claude Garamond.
Known for its elegance and readability, Garamond
remains a standard for book typography.

Cover art by Stephanie Wilson. Cover design by Stefanie Morejon.

Printed in the United States of America, and Canada.

www.ingramcontent.com/pod-product-compliance
Lightning Source LLC
Chambersburg PA
CBHW052013240626
47153CB00008B/2862